His gaze settled on her. As their eyes met across the drive, Jo felt...disoriented. Looking at Phillip Beaumont was one thing, but apparently being looked at by Phillip Beaumont?

Something else entirely.

Heat flushed her face as the corner of his mouth curved up into a smile. She couldn't pull away from his gaze. He looked like he was glad to see her—which she knew wasn't possible. He had no idea who she was and couldn't have been expecting her. Besides, compared to his traveling companions, no one in their right mind would even notice her.

But that look...

Happy and hungry and relieved. Like he'd come all this way just to see her, and now that she was here, the world would be right again.

No one had looked at her like that. Ever.

* * *

Tempted by a Cowboy
is part of The Beaumont Heirs trilogy:
One Colorado family, limitless scandal!

* * *

If you're on Twitter,
tell us what you think of Harlequin Desire!
#harlequindesire

Dear Reader,

Welcome back to Colorado! The Beaumonts are one of Denver's oldest, most preeminent families. The Beaumont Heirs are the children of Hardwick Beaumont, the third generation to run the Beaumont Brewery, world-famous for the team of Percherons that pulls the Beaumont wagon in commercials and parades.

Although he's been dead for almost a decade, Hardwick's womanizing ways—the four marriages and divorces, the ten children and uncounted illegitimate children—are still leaving ripples in the Beaumont family.

Phillip Beaumont is the second oldest Beaumont heir. He was ignored by his father and his stepmothers, so he did whatever he wanted. He's a hard-partying playboy—most of the time. But when he goes out to Beaumont Farms, where the storied Percherons are located, he can be something else—a cowboy. Phillip just bought a rare Akhal-Teke horse named Kandar's Golden Sun for the cool price of $7 million!

But Sun isn't right, and Phillip's at his wit's end trying to save the horse. He hires renowned trainer Jo Spears to work her magic on Sun. Jo's got some dark secrets of her own—and she will not let herself be tempted by any man. But the one thing she hasn't counted on is just how tempting Phillip can be!

Tempted by the Cowboy is a sensual story about discovering who you are and falling in love. I hope you enjoy reading this book as much as I enjoyed writing it! For more information about the other Beaumont Heirs, be sure to stop by www.sarahmanderson.com!

Sarah

TEMPTED BY A COWBOY

SARAH M. ANDERSON

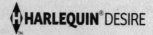

Recycling programs
for this product may
not exist in your area.

ISBN-13: 978-0-373-73346-0

Tempted by a Cowboy

Printed in U.S.A.

www.Harlequin.com

Books by Sarah M. Anderson

Harlequin Desire

A Man of His Word #2130
A Man of Privilege #2171
A Man of Distinction #2184
A Real Cowboy #2211
*Straddling the Line #2232
*Bringing Home the Bachelor #2254
*Expecting a Bolton Baby #2267
What a Rancher Wants #2282
‡Not the Boss's Baby #2328
‡Tempted by a Cowboy #2333

*The Bolton Brothers
‡The Beaumont Heirs

Other titles by this author available in ebook format.

SARAH M. ANDERSON

Award-winning author Sarah M. Anderson may live east of the Mississippi River, but her heart lies out West on the Great Plains. With a lifelong love of horses and two history teachers for parents, she had plenty of encouragement to learn everything she could about the tribes of the Great Plains.

When she started writing, it wasn't long before her characters found themselves out in South Dakota among the Lakota Sioux. She loves to put people from two different worlds into new situations and to see how their backgrounds and cultures take them someplace they never thought they'd go.

Sarah's book *A Man of Privilege* won the *RT Book Reviews* 2012 Reviewers' Choice Best Book Awards Series: Harlequin Desire.

When not helping out at her son's school or walking her rescue dogs, Sarah spends her days having conversations with imaginary cowboys and American Indians, all of which is surprisingly well-tolerated by her wonderful husband. Readers can find out more about Sarah's love of cowboys and Indians at www.sarahmanderson.com.

To Phil Chu, who kept his promise and got me on television—that's what friends are for, right?
I can't believe we've been friends for twenty years!
Here's your book, Phil!

One

Jo got out of the truck and stretched. Man, it'd been a long drive from Kentucky to Denver.

But she'd made it to Beaumont Farms.

Getting this job was a major accomplishment—a vote of confidence that came with the weight of the Beaumont family name behind it.

This wouldn't be just a huge paycheck—the kind that could cover a down payment on a ranch of her own. This was proof that she was a respected horse trainer and her nontraditional methods worked.

A bowlegged man came out of the barn, slapping a pair of gloves against his leg as he walked. Maybe fifty, he had the lined face of a man who'd spent most of his years outside.

He was *not* Phillip Beaumont, the handsome face of the Beaumont Brewery and the man who owned this farm. Even though she shouldn't be, Jo was disappointed.

It was for the best. A man as sinfully good-looking as

Phillip would be…tempting. And she absolutely could not afford to be tempted. Professional horse trainers did not fawn over the people paying their bills—especially when those people were known for their partying ways. Jo did *not* party, not anymore. She was here to do a job and that was that.

"Mr. Telwep?"

"Sure am," the man said, nodding politely. "You the horse whisperer?"

"Trainer," Jo snapped, unable to help herself. She detested being labeled a "whisperer." Damn that book that had made that a thing. "I don't *whisper*. I *train*."

Richard's bushy eyebrows shot up at her tone. She winced. So much for *that* first impression. But she was so used to having to defend her reputation that the reaction was automatic. She put on a friendly smile and tried again. "I'm Jo Spears."

Thankfully, the older man didn't seem too fazed by her lack of social graces. "Miz Spears, call me Richard," he said, coming over to give her a firm handshake.

"Jo," she replied. She liked men like Richard. They'd spent their lives caring for animals. As long as he and his hired hands treated her like a professional, then this would work. "What do you have for me?"

"It's a—well, better to show you."

"Not a Percheron?" The Beaumont Brewery was world-famous for the teams of Percherons that had pulled their wagons in all their commercials for—well, for forever. A stuffed Beaumont Percheron had held a place of honor in the middle of her bed when she'd been growing up.

"Not this time. Even rarer."

Rarer? Not that Percheron horses were rare, but they weren't terribly common in the United States. The massive draft horses had fallen out of fashion now that people weren't using them to pull plows anymore.

"One moment." She couldn't leave Betty in the truck. Not if she didn't want her front seat destroyed, anyway.

Jo opened the door and unhooked Betty's traveling harness. The donkey's ears quivered in anticipation. "Ready to get out?"

Jo scooped Betty up and set her on the ground. Betty let off a serious round of kicks as Richard said, "I heard you traveled with a—well, what the heck is *that?*" with a note of amusement in his voice.

"That," Jo replied, "is Itty Bitty Betty. She's a mini donkey." This was a conversation she'd had many a time. "She's a companion animal."

By this time, Betty had settled down and had begun investigating the grass around her. Barely three feet tall, she was indeed mini. At her size and weight, she was closer to a medium sized dog than a donkey—and acted like it, too. Jo had trained Betty, of course, but the little donkey had been Jo's companion ever since Granny bought Betty for Jo almost ten years ago. Betty had helped Jo crawl out of the darkness. For that, Jo would be forever grateful.

Richard scratched his head in befuddlement at the sight of the pint-size animal. "Danged if I've ever seen a donkey that small. I don't think you'll be wanting to put her in with Sun just yet." He turned and began walking.

Jo perked up. "Sun?" She fell in step with Richard and whistled over her shoulder. Betty came trotting.

"Danged if I've ever," Richard repeated.

"Sun?" she said.

"Kandar's Golden Sun." Richard blew out hard, the frustration obvious. "You ever heard of an Akhal-Teke?"

The name rang a bell. "Isn't that the breed that sired the Arabian?"

"Yup. From Turkmenistan. Only about five thousand in the world." He led the way around the barn to a paddock off to one side, partially shaded by trees.

In the middle of the paddock was a horse that probably *was* golden, as the name implied. But sweat matted his coat and foam dripped from his mouth and neck, giving him a dull, dirty look. The horse was running and bucking in wild circles and had worked himself up to a lather.

"Yup," Richard said, the disappointment obvious in his voice. "That's Kandar's Golden Sun, all right."

Jo watched the horse run. "Why's he so worked up?"

"We moved him from his stall to the paddock. Three hours ago." Jo looked at the older man, but he shrugged. "Took three men. We try to be gentle, but the damn thing takes one look at us and goes ballistic."

Three hours this horse had been bucking and running? Jesus, it was a miracle he hadn't collapsed in a heap. Jo had dealt with her share of terrified horses but sooner or later, they all wore themselves out.

"What happened?"

"That's the thing. No one knows. Mr. Beaumont flew to Turkmenistan himself to look at Sun. He understands horses," Richard added in explanation.

Heat flooded her cheeks. "I'm aware of his reputation."

How could anyone *not* be aware of Phillip Beaumont's reputation? He'd made the *People Magazine* "Most Beautiful" list more than a few years in a row. He had the sort of blond hair that always looked as if he'd walked off a beach, a strong chin and the kind of jaw that could cut stone. He did the Beaumont Brewery commercials but also made headlines on gossip websites and tabloid magazines for some of the stunts he pulled at clubs in Vegas and L.A. Like the time he'd driven a Ferrari into a pool. At the top of a hotel.

No doubt about it, Phillip was a hard-partying playboy. Except…except when he wasn't. In preparing for this job, she'd found an interview he'd done with *Western Horseman* magazine. In that interview—and the accompanying photos—he hadn't been a jaded playboy but an honest-to-God cowboy. He'd talked about horses and herd management and certainly looked like the real McCoy in his boots, jeans, flannel shirt and cowboy hat. He'd said he was building Beaumont Farms as a preeminent stable in the West. Considering the Beaumont family name and its billions in the bank—it wasn't some lofty goal. It was within his reach.

Which one was he? The playboy too sinfully handsome to resist or the hard-working cowboy who wasn't afraid to get dirt on his boots?

No matter which one he was, she was not interested. She couldn't *afford* to be interested in a playboy, especially one who was going to sign her checks. Yes, she'd been training horses for years now, but most wealthy owners of the valuable horses didn't want to take a chance on her nontraditional methods. She'd taken every odd job in every out-of-the-way ranch and farm in the lower forty-eight states to build her clientele. The call from Beaumont Farms was her first major contract with people who bought horses not for thousands of dollars, but for *millions*. If she could save this horse, her reputation would be set.

Besides, the odds of even meeting Phillip Beaumont were slim. Richard was the man she'd be working with. She pulled her thoughts away from the unattainable and focused on why she was here—the horse.

Richard snorted. "We don't deal too much with the partying out here. We just work horses." He waved a hand at Sun, who obliged by rearing on to his back legs and whinnying in panic. "Best we can figure is that maybe something happened on the plane ride? But there were no marks, no wounds. No crashes—not even a rough landing, according to the pilots."

"Just a horse that went off the rails," she said, watching as Sun pawed at the dirt as if he were killing a snake.

"Yup." Richard hung his head. "The horse ain't right but Mr. Beaumont's convinced he can be fixed—a horse to build a stable on, he keeps saying. Spent some ungodly sum of money on him—he'd hate to lose his investment. Personally, I can't stand to see an animal suffer like that. But Mr. Beaumont won't let me put Sun out of his misery. I hired three other trainers before you and none of them lasted a week. You're the horse's last chance. You can't fix him, he'll have to be put down."

This had to be why Richard hadn't gone into specifics over email. He was afraid he'd scare Jo off. "Who'd you hire?"

The older man dug the tip of his boot into the grass. "Lansing, Hoffmire and Callet."

Jo snorted. Lansing was a fraud. Hoffmire was a former farm manager, respected in horse circles. Callet was old-school—and an asshole. He'd tracked her down once to tell her to stay the hell away from his clientele.

She would take particular joy in saving a horse he couldn't.

Moving slowly, she walked to the paddock gate, Betty trotting to keep up. She unhooked the latch on the gate and let it swing open about a foot and a half.

Sun stopped and watched her. Then he *really* began to pitch a fit. His legs flailed as he bucked and reared and slammed his hooves into the ground so hard she felt the shock waves through the dirt. *Hours of this*, Jo thought. *And no one knows why.*

She patted her leg, which was the signal for Betty to stay close. Then Jo stepped into the paddock.

"Miss—" Richard called out, terror in his voice when he realized what she was doing. "Logan, get the tranq gun!"

"Quiet, please." It came out gentle because she was doing her best to project calm.

She heard footsteps—probably Logan and the other

hands, ready to ride to her rescue. She held up a hand, motioning them to stop, and then closed the gate behind her and Betty.

The horse went absolutely wild. It hurt to see an animal so lost in its own hell that there didn't seem to be any way out.

She knew the feeling. It was a hard thing to see, harder to remember the years she'd lost to her own hell.

She'd found her way out. She'd hit bottom so hard it'd almost killed her but through the grace of God, Granny and Itty Bitty Betty, she'd fought her way back out.

She'd made it her life's work to help animals do the same. Even lost causes like Sun could be saved—*not* fixed, because there was no erasing the damage that had already been done. Scars were forever. But moving forward meant accepting the scars. It was that simple. She'd accepted hers.

Jo could stand here for hours listening to the world move, if that was what it took.

It didn't. After what was probably close to forty-five minutes, Sun stopped his frantic pacing. First, he stopped kicking, then he slowed from a run to a trot, then to a walk. Finally, he stood in the middle of the paddock, sides heaving and head down. For the first time, the horse was still.

She could almost hear him say, *I give up.*

It was a low place to be, when living hurt that much.

She understood. She couldn't fix this horse. No one could. But she could save him.

She patted her leg again and turned to walk out of the paddock. A group of seven men stood watching the show Sun had put on for her. Richard had a tranq gun in the hand he was resting on a bar of the paddock.

They were silent. No one shouted about her safety as she turned her back on Sun, no one talked about how the horse must be possessed. They watched her walk to the gate, open it, walk out, and shut it as if they were witnessing a miracle.

"I'll take the job."

Relief so intense it almost knocked her back a step broke over the ranch manager's face. The hired hands all grinned, obviously thankful that Sun was someone else's problem now.

"Provided," she went on, "my conditions are met."

Richard tried to look stern, but he didn't quite make it. "Yeah?"

"I need an on-site hookup for my trailer. That way, if Sun has a problem in the middle of the night, I'm here to deal with it."

"We've got the electric. I'll have Jerry rig up something for the sewer."

"Second, no one else deals with Sun. I feed him, I groom him, I move him. The rest of you stay clear."

"Done," Richard agreed without hesitation. The hands all nodded.

So far, so good. "We do this my way or we don't do it at all. No second-guessing from you, the hired hands or the owners. I won't rush the horse and I expect the same treatment. *And* I expect to be left alone. I don't date or hook up. Clear?"

She hated having to throw that out there because she knew it made her sound as if she thought men would be fighting over her. But she'd done enough harm by hooking up before. Even if she was sober this time, she couldn't risk another life.

Plus, she was a single woman, traveling alone in a trailer with a bed. Some men thought that was enough. Things worked better if everything was cut-and-dried up front.

Richard looked around at his crew. Some were blushing, a few looked bummed—but most of them were just happy that they wouldn't have to deal with Sun anymore.

Then Richard looked across the fields. A long, black limousine was heading toward them.

"Damn," one of the hands said, "the boss."

Everyone but Jo and Richard made themselves scarce. Sun found his second wind and began a full-fledged fit.

"This isn't going to be a problem, is it?" Jo asked Richard, who was busy dusting off his jeans and straightening his shirt.

"Shouldn't be." He did not sound convincing. "Mr. Beaumont wants the best for Sun."

The *but* on the end of that statement was as loud as if Richard had actually said the word. *But* Phillip Beaumont was a known womanizer who made headlines around the world for his conquests.

Richard turned his attention back to her. "You're hired. I'll do my level-best to make sure that Mr. Beaumont stays clear of you."

In other words, Richard had absolutely no control of the situation. A fact that became more apparent as the limo got closer. The older man stood at attention as the vehicle rolled to a stop in front of the barn.

Phillip Beaumont didn't scare her. Or intimidate her. She'd dealt with handsome, entitled men before and none of them had ever tempted her to fall back into her old ways. None of them made her forget the scars. This wouldn't be any different. She was just here for the job.

The limo door opened. A bare, female leg emerged from the limo at the same time as giggling filled the air. Behind her, Jo heard Sun kick it up a notch.

The first leg was followed by a second. Jo wasn't that surprised when a second set of female legs followed the first. By that time, the first woman had stepped clear of the limo's door and Jo could see that, while she was wearing clothing, the dress consisted of little more than a bikini's worth of black sequined material. The second woman stood up and pulled the red velvet material of her skirt down around her hips.

Beside her, Richard made a sound that was stuck somewhere between a sigh and a groan. Jo took that to mean that this wasn't the first time Phillip had shown up with women dressed like hookers.

Betty nickered in boredom and went back to cropping grass. Jo pretty much felt the same way. Of course this was how Phillip Beaumont rolled. Those headlines hadn't lied. The thing that had been less honest had been that interview in *Western Horseman*. That had probably been more about rehabilitating his brand image than about his actual love and respect for horses.

But on the bright side, if he'd brought his own entertainment to the ranch, he'd leave her to her work. That's what was important here—she had to save Sun, cement her reputation as a horse trainer and add this paycheck to the fund that she'd use to buy her own ranch. Adding Beaumont Farms to her résumé was worth putting up with the hassle of, well, *this*.

Then another set of legs appeared. Unlike the first sets, these legs were clad in what looked like expensive Italian leather shoes and fine-cut wool trousers. Phillip Beaumont himself stood and looked at his farm over the top of the limo, all blond hair and gleaming smile. He wore an odd look on his face. He almost looked *relieved*.

His gaze settled on her. As their eyes met across the drive, Jo felt…disoriented. Looking at Phillip Beaumont was one thing, but apparently being looked at by Phillip Beaumont?

Something else entirely.

Heat flushed her face as the corner of his mouth curved up into a smile, grabbed hold of her and refused to let her go. She couldn't pull away from his gaze—and she wasn't sure she wanted to. He looked as if he was glad to see her—which she knew wasn't possible. He had no idea who she was and couldn't have been expecting her. Besides, compared to his traveling companions, no one in their right mind would even notice her.

But that look…. Happy and hungry and *relieved*. Like he'd come all this way just to see her and now that she was here, the world would be right again.

No one had looked at her like that. *Ever*. Before, when she'd been a party girl, men looked at her with a wolfish hunger that had very little to do with her as a woman and everything to do with them wanting to get laid. And since the accident? Well, she wore her hair like this and dressed like she did specifically so she wouldn't invite people to look at her.

He saw right through her.

The women lost their balance and nearly tumbled to the ground, but Phillip caught them in his arms. He pulled them apart and settled one on his left side, the other on his right. The women giggled, as if this were nothing but hilarious.

It hurt to see them, like ghosts of her past come back to haunt her.

"Mr. Beaumont," Richard began in a warm, if desperate, tone as he went to meet his boss. "We weren't expecting you today."

"Dick," Phillip said, which caused his traveling companions to break out into renewed giggles. "I wanted to show my new friends—" He looked down at Blonde Number One.

"Katylynn," Number One giggled. Of course.

"Sailor," Number Two helpfully added.

Phillip's head swung up in a careful arc, another disarming smile already in place as he gave the girls a squeeze. "I wanted to show Sun to Katylynn and Sailor."

"Mr. Beaumont," Richard began again. Jo heard more anger in his voice this time. "Sun is not—"

"Wha's wrong with that horse?" Sailor took a step away from Phillip and pointed at Sun.

They all turned to look. Sun was now bucking with renewed vigor. *Damn stamina*, Jo thought as she watched him.

"Wha's making him do that?" Katylynn asked.

"You are," Jo informed the trio.

The women glared at her. "Who are you?" Sailor asked in a haughty tone.

"Yes, who are you?" Phillip Beaumont spoke slowly—carefully—as his eyes focused on her again.

Again, her face prickled with unfamiliar heat. *Get ahold of yourself*, she thought, forcibly breaking the eye contact. She wasn't the kind of woman who got drunk and got lost in a man's eyes. Not anymore. She'd left that life behind and no one—not even someone as handsome and rich as Phillip Beaumont—would tempt her back to it.

"Mr. Beaumont, this here is Jo Spears. She's the horse…" She almost heard *whisperer* sneak out through his teeth. "Trainer. The new trainer for Sun."

She gave Richard an appreciative smile. A quick study, that one.

Phillip detached himself from his companions, which led to them making whimpering noises of protest.

As Phillip closed the distance between him and Jo, that half-smile took hold of his mouth again. He stopped with two feet still between them. "You're the new trainer?"

She stared at his eyes. They were pale green with flecks of gold around the edges. *Nice eyes.*

Nice eyes that bounced. It wasn't a big movement, but Phillip's eyes were definitely moving of their own accord. She knew the signs of intoxication and that one was a dead giveaway. He was drunk.

She had to admire his control, though. Nothing else in his mannerisms or behaviors gave away that he was three sheets to the wind. Which really only meant one thing.

Being this drunk wasn't something new for him. He'd gotten very good at masking his state. That was something that took years of practice.

She'd gotten good at it, too—but it was so exhausting to keep up that false front of competency, to act normal when she wasn't. She'd hated being that person. She wasn't anymore.

She let this realization push down on the other part of her brain that was still admiring his lovely eyes. Phillip Beaumont represented every single one of her triggers wrapped up in one extremely attractive package. Everything she could never be again if she wanted to be a respected horse trainer, not an out-of-control alcoholic.

She *needed* this job, needed the prestige of retraining a horse like Sun on her résumé and the paycheck that went with it. She absolutely could not allow a handsome man who could hold his liquor to tempt her back into a life she'd long since given up.

She did not hook up. Not even with the likes of Phillip Beaumont.

"I'm just here for the horse," she told him.

He tilted his head in what looked like acknowledgement without breaking eye contact and without losing that smile.

Man, this was unnerving. Men who looked at her usually saw the bluntly cut, shoulder-length hair and the flannel shirts and the jeans and dismissed her out of hand. That was how she wanted it. It kept a safe distance between her and the rest of the world. That was just the way it had to be.

But this look was doing some very unusual things to her. Things she didn't like. Her cheeks got hot—was she blushing?—and a strange prickling started at the base of her neck and raced down her back.

She gritted her teeth but thankfully, he was the one who broke the eye contact first. He looked down at Betty, still blissfully cropping grass. "And who is this?"

Jo braced herself. "This is Itty Bitty Betty, my companion mini donkey."

Instead of the lame joke or snorting laughter, Phillip leaned down, held his hand out palm up and let Betty sniff his hand. "Well hello, Little Bitty Betty. Aren't you a good girl?"

Jo decided not to correct him on her name. It wasn't worth it. What was worth it, though, was the way Betty snuffled at his hand and then let him rub her ears.

That weird prickling sensation only got stronger as she watched Phillip Beaumont make friends with her donkey. "We've got nice grass," he told her, sounding for all the world as if he was talking to a toddler. "You'll like it here."

Jo realized she was staring at Phillip with her mouth open, which she quickly corrected. The people who hired her usually made a joke about Betty or stated they weren't paying extra for a donkey of any size. But Phillip?

Wearing a smile that bordered on cute he looked up at Jo as Betty went back to the grass. "She's a good companion, I can tell."

She couldn't help herself. "Can you?"

Richard had said his boss was a good judge of horses. He'd certainly sounded as if were true it in that interview. She wanted him to be a good judge of horses, to be a real person and not just a shallow, beer-peddling facade of a man. Even though she had no right to want that from him, she did.

His smile went from adorable to wicked in a heartbeat and damned if other parts of her body didn't start prickling at the sight. "I'm an *excellent* judge of character."

Right then, the party girls decided to speak up. "Philly, we want to go home," one cooed.

"With you," the other one added.

"Yes," Jo told him, casting a glare back at the women. "I can see that."

Sun made an unholy noise behind them. Richard shouted and the blondes screamed.

Jesus, Jo thought as Sun pawed at the ground and then charged the paddock fence, snot streaming out of his nose. If he hit the fence at that speed, there wouldn't be anything left to save.

Everyone else dove out of the way. Jo turned and ran toward the horse, throwing her hands up and shouting "Hiyahh!" at the top of her lungs.

It worked with feet to spare. Sun spooked hard to the left and only hit the paddock fence with his hindquarters—which might be enough to bruise him but wouldn't do any other damage.

"Jesus," she said out loud as the horse returned to his bucking. Her chest heaved as the adrenaline pumped through her body.

"I'll tranq him," Richard said beside her, leveling the gun at Sun.

"No." She pushed the muzzle away before he could squeeze the trigger. "Leave him be. He started this, he's got to finish it."

Richard gave her a hell of a doubtful look. "We'll have to tranq him to get him back to his stall. I can't afford anymore workman's comp because of this horse."

She turned to give the ranch manager her meanest look. "We do this my way or we don't do it at all. That was the deal. I say you don't shoot him. Leave him in this paddock. Set out hay and water. No one else touches this horse. Do I make myself clear?"

"Do what she says," Phillip said behind her.

Jo turned back to the paddock to make sure that Sun hadn't decided to exit on the other side. Nope. Just more bucking circles. It'd almost been a horse's version of *shut the hell up*. She grinned at him. On that point, she had to agree.

She could feel her connection with Sun start to grow, which was a good thing. The more she could understand what he was thinking, the easier it would be to help him.

"Philly, we want to go," one of the blondes demanded with a full-on whine.

"Fine," Phillip snapped. "Ortiz, make sure the ladies get back to their homes."

A different male voice—probably the limo driver—said, "Yes sir, Mr. Beaumont." This announcement was met with cries of protest, which quickly turned to howls of fury.

Jo didn't watch. She kept her eye on Sun, who was still freaking out at all the commotion. If he made another bolt for the fence, she might have to let Richard tranq him and she really didn't want that to happen. Shots fired now would only make her job that much harder in the long run.

Finally, the limo doors shut and she heard the car drive off. Thank God. With the women gone, the odds that Sun would settle down were a lot better.

She heard footsteps behind her and tensed. She didn't want Phillip to touch her. She'd meant what she'd said to the hired hands earlier—she didn't hook up with anyone. Especially not men like Phillip Beaumont. She couldn't afford to have her professional reputation compromised, not when she'd finally gotten a top-tier client—and a horse no one else could save. She needed this job far more than she needed Phillip Beaumont to smile at her.

He came level with her and stopped. He was too close—more than close enough to touch.

She panicked. "I don't sleep with clients," she announced into the silence—and immediately felt stupid.

She was letting a little thing like prickling heat undermine her authority here. She was a horse trainer. That was all.

"I'll be sure to take that into consideration." He looked down at her and turned on the most seductive smile she'd ever seen.

Oh, what a smile. She struggled for a moment to remember why, exactly, she didn't need that smile in her life. How long had it been since she'd let herself smile back at a man? How long had it been since she'd allowed herself even a little bit of fun?

Years. But then the skin on the back of her neck pulled and she remembered the hospital and the pain. The scars. She hadn't gotten this job because she smiled at attractive men. She'd gotten this job because she was a horse trainer who could save a broken horse.

She was a professional, by God. When she'd made her announcement to the hired hands earlier, they'd all nodded and agreed. But Phillip?

He looked as if she'd issued a personal challenge. One that he was up to meeting.

Heat flushed her face as she fluttered—honest-to-God fluttered. One little smile—that wouldn't cost her too much, would it?

No.

She pushed back against whatever insanity was gripping her. She no longer fluttered. She did not fall for party boys. She did not sleep with men at the drop of a hat because they were cute or bought her drinks. She did not look for a human connection in a bar because the connections she'd always made there were never very human.

She would not be tempted by Phillip Beaumont. It didn't matter how tempting he was. She would not smile back because one smile would lead to another and she couldn't let that happen.

He notched up one eyebrow as if he were acknowledging how much he'd flustered her. But instead of saying something else, he walked past her and leaned heavily against the paddock fence, staring at Sun. His body language pulled at her in ways she didn't like. So few of the people who hired her to train horses actually cared about their animals. They looked at the horse and saw dollars—either in money spent, money yet to be made, or insurance payments. That's why she didn't get involved with her clients. She could count the exceptions on one hand, like Whitney Maddox, a horse breeder she'd stayed with a few months last winter. But those cases were few and far between and never involved men with reputations like Phillip Beaumont.

But the way Phillip was looking at his horse… There was a pain in his face that seemed to mirror what the horse was feeling. It was a hard thing to see.

No. She was not going to feel sorry for this poor little rich boy. She'd come from nothing, managed to nearly destroy her own life and actually managed to make good all by herself.

"He's a good horse—I know he is." Phillip didn't even glance in her direction. He sounded different now that the ladies were gone. It was almost as if she could see his mask slip. What was left was a man who was tired and worried. "I know Richard thinks he should be put out of his misery, but I can't do it. I can't—I can't give up on him. If he could just…" He scrubbed a hand through his hair, which, damn it, only made it look better. He turned to her. "Can you fix him?"

"No," she told him. What was left of his playboy mask fell completely away at this pronouncement.

In that moment, Jo saw something else in Phillip Beaumont's eyes—something that she didn't just recognize, but that she understood.

He was *so* lost. Just like she'd been once.

"I can't fix him—but I can save him."

He looked at her. "There's a difference?"

"Trust me—all the difference in the world."

Jo looked back at Sun, who was quickly working through his energy. Soon, he'd calm down. Maybe he'd even drink some water and sleep. That'd be good. She wanted to save him in a way that went beyond the satisfaction of a job well done or the fees that Phillip Beaumont could afford to pay her.

She wanted to save this horse because once, she'd hurt as much as he did right now. And no one—no horse— should hurt that much. Not when she could make it better.

She wasn't here for Phillip Beaumont. He might be a scarred man in a tempting package, but she'd avoided temptation before and she'd do it again.

"Don't give up on him," he said in a voice that she wasn't sure was meant for her.

"Don't worry," she told the horse as much as she told Phillip. "I won't."

She would *not* give up on the horse.

She wasn't sure she had such high hopes for the man.

Two

Light. Too much light.

God, his head.

Phillip rolled away from the sunlight but moving his head did not improve the situation. In fact, it only made things worse.

Finally, he sat up, which had the benefit of getting the light out of his face but also made his stomach roll. He managed to get his eyes cracked open. He wasn't in his downtown apartment and he wasn't in his bedroom at the Beaumont Mansion.

The walls of the room were rough-cut logs, the fireplace was stone and a massive painting showing a pair of Percherons pulling a covered wagon across the prairie hung over the mantle.

Ah. He was at the farm. Immediately, his stomach unclenched. There were a lot worse places to wake up. He knew that from experience. Back when his grandfather had built it, it'd been little more than a cabin set far away from the world of beer. John Beaumont hadn't wasted money on opulence where no one would see it. That's why the Beaumont Mansion was a work of art and the farm was…not.

Phillip liked it out here. Over the years, the original cabin had been expanded, but always with the rough-hewn logs. His room was a part he'd added himself, mostly because he wanted a view and a deck to look at it from. The hot tub outside didn't hurt, either, but unlike the hot tub at his bachelor pad, this one was mostly for soaking.

Mostly. He was Phillip Beaumont, after all.

Phillip sat in bed for a while, rubbing his temples and trying to sift through the random memories from the last few days. He knew he'd had an event in Las Vegas on… Thursday. That'd been a hell of a night.

He was pretty sure he'd had a club party in L.A. on Friday, hadn't he? No, that wasn't right. Beaumont Brewery had a big party tent at a music festival and Phillip had been there for the Friday festivities. Lots of music people. *Lots* of beer.

And Saturday…he'd been back in Denver for a private party for some guy's twenty-first birthday. But, no matter how hard he tried to remember the party, his brain wouldn't supply any details.

So, did that mean today was Sunday or Monday? Hell, he didn't know. That was the downside of his job. Phillip was vice president of Marketing in charge of special events for Beaumont Brewery, which loosely translated into making sure everyone had a good time at a Beaumont-sponsored event and talked about it on social media.

Phillip was very good at his job.

He found the clock. It was 11:49. He needed to get up. The sun was only getting brighter. Why didn't he have room-darkening blinds in here?

Oh, yeah. Because the windows opened up on to a beautiful vista, full of lush grass, tall trees and his horses. Damn his aesthetic demands.

He got his feet swung over the bed and under him. Each movement was like being hit with a meat cleaver right between the eyes. Yeah, that must have been one *hell* of a party.

He navigated a flight of stairs and two hallways to the kitchen, which was in the original building. He got the coffee going and then dug a sports drink out of the fridge. He popped some Tylenol and guzzled the sports drink.

Almost immediately, his head felt better. He finished the first bottle and cracked open a second. Food. He needed food. But he needed a shower first.

Phillip headed back to his bathroom. That was the other reason he'd built his own addition—the other bathroom held the antique claw-foot tub that couldn't hope to contain all six of his feet.

His bathroom had a walk-in shower, a separate tub big enough for two and a double sink that stretched out for over eight feet. He could sprawl out all over the place and still have room to spare.

He soaked his head in cool water, which got his blood pumping again. He'd always had a quick recovery time from a good party—today was no different.

Finally, he got dressed in his work clothes and went back to the kitchen. He made some eggs, which helped his stomach. The coffee was done, so he filled up a thermal mug and added a shot of whiskey. Hair of the dog.

Finally, food in his stomach and coffee in his hand, he found his phone and scrolled through it.

Ah. It was Monday. Which meant he had no recollection of Sunday. Damn.

He didn't dwell on that. Instead, he scrolled through his contacts list. Lots of new numbers. Not too many pictures. One he'd apparently already posted to Instagram of him and Drake on stage together? Cool. That was a dream-come-true kind of moment right there. He was thrilled someone had gotten a photo of it.

He scanned some of the gossip sites. There were mentions of the clubs, the festival—but nothing terrible. Mostly just who's-who tallies and some wild speculation about who went to bed with whom.

Phillip heaved a sigh of relief. He'd done his job well. He always did. People had a good time, drank a lot of Beaumont Beer and talked the company up to their friends. And they did that because Phillip brought all the elements together for them—the beer, the party, the celebrities.

It was just that sometimes, people talked about things that gave the PR department fits. No matter how many times Phillip tried to tell those suits who worked for his brother Chadwick that there was no such thing as bad PR, every time he made headlines for what they considered the "wrong" reasons, Chadwick felt the need to have a coming-to-Jesus moment with Phillip about how his behavior was damaging the brand name and costing the company money and blah, blah, blah.

Frankly, Phillip could do with less Chadwick in his life.

That wasn't going to happen this week, thank God. The initial summaries looked good—the Klout Score was up, the hits were high and on Saturday, the Beaumont party tent had been trending for about four hours on Twitter.

Phillip shut off his phone with a smile. That was a job well done in his book.

He felt human again. His head was clearing and the food in his stomach was working. *Hair of the dog always does the trick*, he thought as he refilled his mug and put on his boots. He felt good.

He was happy to be back on the farm in a way he couldn't quite put into words. He missed his horses—especially Sun. He hadn't seen Sun in what felt like weeks.

The last he knew, Richard had hired some trainer who'd promised to fix the horse. But that was a while ago. Maybe a month?

There it was again—that uneasy feeling that had nothing to do with the hangover or the breakfast. He didn't like that feeling, so he took an extra big swig of coffee to wash it away.

He had some time before the next round of events kicked off. There was a lull between now and Spring Break. That was fine by Phillip. He would get caught up with Richard, evaluate his horses, go for some long rides—hopefully on Sun—and ignore the world for a while. Then, by the time he was due to head south to help ensure that Beaumont Beers were the leading choice of college kids everywhere, he'd be good to go. Brand loyalty couldn't start early enough.

He grabbed his hat off the peg by the door and headed down to the barn. The half-mile walk did wonders for his head. The whole place was turning green as the last of the winter gave way to spring. Daffodils popped up in random spots and the pastures were so bright they hurt his eyes.

It felt good to be home. He needed a week or two to recover, that was all.

As he rounded the bend in the road that connected the house to the main barn, he saw that Sun was out in a paddock. That was a good sign. As best he could recall, Richard had said they couldn't move the horse out of his stall without risking life and limb. Phillip had nearly had his own head taken off by a flying hoof the one time he'd tried to put a halter on his own horse—something that Sun had let him do when they were at the stables in Turkmenistan.

God, he wished he knew where things had gone wrong. Sun had been a handful, that was for sure—but at his old stables, he'd been manageable. Phillip had even inquired into bringing his former owner out to the farm to see if the old man who spoke no English would be able to settle Sun down. The man had refused.

But if that last trainer had worked wonders, then Phillip could get on with his plan. The trainer's services had cost a fortune, but if he'd gotten Sun back on track, it was worth it. The horse's bloodlines could be traced back on paper to the 1880s and the former owner had transcribed an oral bloodline that went back to the 1600s. True, an oral bloodline didn't count much, but Philip knew Sun was a special horse. His ancestors had taken home gold, the Grand Prix de Dressage and too many long-distance races to count.

He needed to highlight Sun's confirmation and stamina—that was what would sell his lineage as a stud. Sun's line would live on for a long time to come. That stamina—and his name—was what breeders would pay top dollar for. But beyond that, there was something noble about the whole thing. The Akhal-Tekes were an ancient breed of horse—the founder of the modern lines of the Arabians and Thoroughbreds. It seemed a shame that almost no one had ever heard of them. They were amazing animals—almost unbreakable, especially compared to the delicate racing Thoroughbreds whose legs seemed to shatter with increasing frequency on the racetrack. A horse like Sun could reinvigorate lines—leading to stronger, faster racehorses.

Phillip felt lighter than he had in a while. Sun was a damned fine horse—the kind of stud upon which to found a line. He must be getting old because as fun as the parties obviously were—photos didn't lie—he was getting to the point where he just wanted to train his horses.

Of course he knew he couldn't hide out here forever. He had a job to do. Not that he needed the money, but working for the Beaumont Brewery wasn't just a family tradition. It was also a damned good way to keep Chadwick off his back. No matter what his older brother said, Phillip wasn't wasting the family fortune on horses and women. He was an important part of the Beaumont brand name—that *more* than offset his occasional forays into horses.

Phillip saw a massive trailer parked off to the side of the barn with what looked like a garden hose and—was that an extension cord?—running from the barn to the trailer. Odd. Had he invited someone out to the farm? Usually, when he had guests, they stayed at the house.

He took a swig of coffee. He didn't like that unsettling feeling of not knowing what was going on.

As he got closer, he saw that Sun wasn't grazing. He was running. That wasn't a good sign.

Sun wasn't better. He was the same. God, what a depressing thought.

Then Phillip saw her. It was obvious she was a *her*— tall, clad in snug jeans and a close-fit flannel shirt, he could see the curve of her hips at three hundred yards. Longish hair hung underneath a brown hat. She sure as hell didn't look like the kind of woman he brought home with him— not even to the farm. So what was she doing here?

Standing in the middle of the paddock while Sun ran in wild circles, that's what.

Phillip shook his head. This had to be a post-hangover hallucination. If Sun weren't better, why would *anyone* be in a paddock with him? The horse was too far gone. It wasn't safe. The horse had knocked a few of the hired hands out of commission for a while. The medical bills were another thing Chadwick rode his ass about.

Not only did the vision of this woman not disperse, but Phillip noticed something else that couldn't be real. Was that a donkey in there with her? He was pretty sure he'd remember buying a donkey that small.

He looked the woman over again, hoping for some sign of recognition. Nothing. He was sure he'd remember thighs and a backside like that. Maybe she'd look different up close.

He walked the rest of the way down to the paddock, his gaze never leaving her. No, she wasn't his type, but variety was the spice of life, wasn't it?

"Good morning," he said in a cheerful voice as he leaned against the fence.

Her back stiffened but she gave no other sign that she'd heard him. The small donkey craned its neck around to give him a look that could only be described as *doleful* as Sun went from a bucking trot to a rearing, snorting mess in seconds.

Jesus, that horse could kill her. But he tried not to let the panic creep into his voice. "Miss, I don't think it's safe to be in there right now." Sun made a sound that was closer to a scream than a whinny. Phillip winced at the noise.

The woman's head dropped in what looked like resignation. Then she patted the side of her leg as she turned and began a slow walk back to the gate. Betty followed close on her heels.

The donkey's name was Betty. How did he know that?

Oh, crap—he *did* know her. Had she been at the party? Had they slept together? He didn't remember seeing any signs of a female in his room or in the house.

He watched as she walked toward him. She was a cowgirl, that much was certain—and not one of those fake ones whose hats were covered in rhinestones and whose jeans had never seen a saddle. The brown hat fit low on her forehead, the flannel shirt was tucked in under a worn leather belt that had absolutely no adornment and her chest—

Phillip was positive he'd remember spending a little quality time with that chest. Despite the nearly unisex clothing, the flannel shirt did nothing to hide the generous breasts that swelled outward, begging him to notice them. Which he did, of course. But he could control his baser urges to ogle a woman. So, after a quick glance at what had to be perfection in breast form, he snapped his eyes up to her face. The movement made his head swim.

It'd be *so* nice if he could remember her, because she was certainly a memorable woman. Her face wasn't made up or altered. She had tanned skin, a light dusting of freckles and a nose that looked as if it might have been broken once. It should have made her look awkward, but he decided it was fitting. There was a certain beauty in the imperfect.

Then she raised her eyes to his and he felt rooted to the spot. Her eyes were clear and bright, a soft hazel. He could get lost in eyes like that.

Not that he got the chance. She scowled at him. The shock of someone other than Chadwick looking so displeased with him put Phillip on the defensive. Still, she was a woman and women were his specialty. So he waited until she'd made it out of the gate and closed it behind Betty.

Once the gate clicked, she didn't head for where he stood. Instead, she went back to ignoring him entirely as she propped a booted foot up on the gate and watched the show Sun was putting on for them.

What. The. Hell.

He was going to have to amend his previous statement—*most* women were his specialty.

Time to get back to basics. One compliment, coming right up. "I don't think I've ever seen anyone wear a pair of jeans like you do." That should do the trick.

Or it would have for any other woman. Instead, she dropped her forehead onto the top bar of the gate—a similar motion to the one she'd made out in the paddock moments ago. Then she turned her face to him. "Was it worth it?"

His generous smile faltered. "Was what worth it?"

Her soft eyes didn't seem so soft anymore. "The blackout. Was it worth it?"

"I have no idea what you're talking about."

That got a smirk out of her, just a small curve of her lips. It was gone in a flash. "That's the definition of a blackout, isn't it? You have no idea who I am or what I'm doing here, do you?"

Sun made that unholy noise again. Phillip tensed. The woman he didn't know looked at the horse and shook her head as if the screaming beast was a disappointment to her. Then she looked at Phillip and shook her head again.

Unfamiliar anger coursed through him, bringing a new clarity to his thoughts. Who the hell was this woman, anyway? "I know you shouldn't be climbing into the paddock with Sun. He's dangerous."

Another smirk. Was she challenging him?

"But he wasn't when you bought him, was he?"

How did she know about that? An idea began to take shape in his mind like a Polaroid developing. He shook his head, hoping the image would get clearer—fast. It didn't. "No."

She stared at him a moment longer. It shouldn't bother him that she knew who he was. Everyone knew who he was. That went with being the face of the Beaumont Brewery.

But she didn't look at him like everyone else did—with that gleam of delight that went with meeting a celebrity in the flesh. Instead, she just looked disappointed.

Well, she could just keep on looking disappointed. He turned his attention to the most receptive being here—the donkey. "How are you this morning, Betty?"

When the woman didn't correct him, he grinned. He'd gotten that part right, at least.

He rubbed the donkey behind the ears, which resulted

in her leaning against his legs and groaning in satisfaction. "Good girl, aren't you?" he whispered.

Maybe he'd have to get a little donkey like this. If Betty wasn't his already.

Maybe, a quiet voice in the back of his head whispered, that blackout *wasn't* worth it.

He took another swig of coffee.

He looked back at the woman. Her posture hadn't changed, but everything about her face had. Instead of a smirk, she was smiling at him—him and the donkey.

The donkey was hers, he realized. And since he already knew the donkey's name, he must have met the woman, too.

Double damn.

That's when he realized he was smiling back at her. What had been superior about her had softened into something that looked closer to delight.

He forgot about not knowing who she was, how she got here or what she was doing with his prize stallion. All he could think was that *now* things were about to get interesting. This was a dance he could do with his eyes closed—a beautiful woman, a welcoming smile—a good time soon to be had by all.

Genuine compliment, take two. "She's a real sweetie, isn't she? I've never seen a donkey this well-behaved." He took a risk. "You did an amazing job training her."

Oh, yeah, that worked much better than the jeans comment had. Her smile deepened as she tilted her head to one side. Soft morning light warmed her face and suddenly, she looked like a woman who wanted to be kissed.

Whoever she was, this woman was unlike anyone he'd ever met before. Different could be good. Hell, different could be great. She wasn't a woman who belonged at the clubs but then, he wasn't at the clubs. He was at his farm and this woman clearly fit in this world.

Maybe he'd enjoy this break from big-city living more than he'd thought he would. After all, his bed was more than large enough to accommodate two people. So was the hot tub.

Yes, the week was suddenly looking up.

But she still hadn't told him who the hell she was and that was becoming a problem. Kissing an anonymous woman in a dark club? No problem. Kissing a cowgirl who was inexplicably on his ranch in broad daylight? Problem.

He had to bite the bullet and admit he didn't remember her name. So, still rubbing Betty's ears, he stuck out a hand. "We got off to a rough beginning." He could only assume that was true, as she'd opened with a blackout comment. "Let's start over. I'm Phillip Beaumont. And you are?"

Some of her softness faded, but she shook his hand with the kind of grip that made it clear she was used to working with her hands. "Jo Spears."

That didn't ring a single damned bell in his head.

It was only after she'd let go of his hand that she added, with a grin that bordered on cruel, "I'm here to retrain Sun."

Three

"*You're* the new trainer?"

Jo fought hard to keep the grin off her face. She wasn't entirely sure she succeeded. Even yesterday, when he'd been toasted, she hadn't been able to surprise Phillip Beaumont. But she'd caught him off guard this morning.

How bad was his hangover? It had to be killer. She could smell whiskey from where she stood. But she would have never guessed it just by looking at him. Hell, his eyes weren't even bloodshot. He had a three-day-old scruff on his cheeks that should have looked messy but, on him, made him look better—like a man who worked with his hands.

Other than that…she let her eyes drift over his body. The jeans weren't the fancy kind that he'd spent hundreds of dollars to make look old and broken in—they looked like the kind he'd broken in himself. The denim work shirt was much the same. Yes, his brown boots had probably cost a pretty penny once—but they were scuffed and scratched, not polished to a high shine. These were his work clothes and he was clearly comfortable in them.

The suit he'd had on yesterday had been the outfit of the Phillip Beaumont who went to parties and did commercials. But the Phillip Beaumont who was petting Betty's ears today?

This was a cowboy. A real one.

Heat flooded her body. She forced herself to ignore it. She would not develop a crush or an infatuation or even an *admiration* for Phillip Beaumont just because he looked good in jeans.

She'd been right about him. He had no memory of yesterday and he'd spiked his coffee this morning. He was everything she couldn't allow herself, all wrapped up in one attractive package. She had a job to do. And if she did it well, a reference from Phillip Beaumont would be worth its weight in gold. It'd be worth that smile of his.

"I believe," she said with a pointed tone that let him know he wasn't fooling anyone, "that we established our identities yesterday afternoon."

The change was impressive. It only took a matter of seconds for his confusion to be buried beneath a warm smile. "Forgive me." He managed to look appropriately contrite while also adding a bit of smolder to his eyes. The effect was almost heady. She was *not* falling for this. Not at all. "I'm just a little surprised. The other trainers have been…"

"Older? Male? Richard told me about his previous attempts." She turned her attention back to the horse to hide her confusion. She could not flutter. Too much was at risk here.

Sun did seem to be calming down. Which meant he hadn't made that screaming noise in a couple of minutes. He was still racing as if his life depended on it, though. "I think it's clear that Sun needs something else."

"And that's you?" He kept his tone light and conversational, but she could hear the doubt lurking below the surface.

The other three men had all been crusty old farts, men who'd been around horses their whole lives. Not like her. "Yup. That's me."

Phillip leaned against the paddock fence. Jo did not like how aware of his body she was. He kicked a foot up on the lowest railing and draped his arms over the top of the fence. It was all very casual—and close enough to touch.

"So what's your plan to fix him?"

She sighed. "As I told you yesterday, I don't fix horses. No one can fix him."

She managed to keep the crack about whether or not he'd remember this conversation tomorrow to herself. She was already pushing her luck with him and she knew it. He was still paying her and, given how big a mess Sun was, she might have enough to put a down payment on her own ranch after this.

Wouldn't that be the ultimate dream? A piece of land to call her own, where the Phillip Beaumonts of the world would bring her their messed-up horses. She wouldn't have to spend days driving across country and showering in a trailer. Betty could run wild and free on her own grass. Her own ranch would be safety and security and she wouldn't have to deal with people at all. Just horses. That's what this job could give to her.

That's why she needed to work extra hard on keeping her distance from the man who was *still* close enough to touch.

He ignored the first part of the statement. "Then what do you do?"

There was no way to sum up what she did. So she didn't. "Save him."

Because she was so aware of Phillip's body, she felt the

tension take hold of him. She turned her head just enough to look at him out of the corner of her eye. Phillip's gaze was trained on the half-crazed horse in the paddock. He looked stricken, as if her words had sliced right through all his charm and left nothing but a raw, broken man who owned a raw, broken horse.

Then he looked at her. His eyes—God, there was so much going on under the surface. She felt herself start to get lost in them, but Sun whinnied, pulling her back to herself.

She could not get lost in Phillip Beaumont. To do so would be to take that first slippery step back down the slope to lost nights and mornings in strangers' beds. And there would be no coming back from that this time.

So she said, in a low voice, "I *only* save horses."

"I don't need to be saved, thank you very much."

Again, the change was impressive. The warm smile that bordered on teasing snapped back onto his face and the honest pain she'd seen in his eyes was gone beneath a wink and twinkle.

She couldn't help it. She looked at his coffee mug. "If you say so."

His grip tightened on the handle, but that was the only sign he'd gotten her meaning. He probably thought the smell of the coffee masked the whiskey. Maybe it did for regular folks, but not for her.

"How are you going to *save* my horse then?" It came out in the same voice he might use to ask a woman on a date.

It was time to end this conversation before things went completely off the rails. "One day at a time."

Let's see if he catches that, she thought as she opened the gate and slowly walked back into the paddock, Betty trailing at her heels.

As she closed the gate behind her, she heard Richard come out of the barn. "Mr. Beaumont—you're up!"

Good. She wanted more time with Sun alone. The horse had almost calmed down before Phillip showed up. If she could get the animal to stay at a trot…

That wasn't happening now. Sun clearly did not like Richard, probably because the older man had been the one to tranquilize him and move him around the most. She was encouraged that, although the horse did freak out any time Phillip showed up, he had sort of settled down this morning as she and Phillip had talked in conversational tones. Sun didn't have any negative associations with Phillip—he just didn't like change. That was a good thing to know.

"Just getting to know the new trainer," Phillip said behind her. She had to give him credit, he managed not to make it sound dismissive.

"If you two are going to talk," she said in a low voice that carried a great distance, "please do so elsewhere. You're freaking out the horse."

There was a pause and she got the feeling that both men were looking at her. Then Richard said, "Now that you're here, I'd like you to see the new Percheron foals." That was followed by the sounds of footsteps leading away from the paddock.

But they weren't far away when she heard Phillip say, "Are you sure about her?"

Jo tensed.

Richard, bless his crusty old heart, came to her defense. As his voice trailed off, she heard him reply, "She came highly recommended. If anyone can fix Sun… She's our last chance."

She couldn't fix this horse. She couldn't fix the man, either, but she had no interest in trying. She would not be swayed by handsome faces, broken-in jeans or kind words for Betty.

She was just here for the horse.

She needed to remember that.

* * *

Phillip woke up early the next day and he knew why. He was hoping there'd be a woman with an attitude standing in a paddock this morning.

Jo Spears. She was not his type—not physically, not socially. Not even close. He sure as hell remembered her today. How could he have forgotten meeting her the day before? That didn't matter. What mattered now was that he was dying to see if she was still in that arena, just standing there.

He hurried through his shower while the coffee brewed. He added a shot of whiskey to keep the headache away and then got a mug for her. While he was at it, he grabbed a couple of carrots from the fridge for the donkey.

Would Jo still be standing in the middle of that paddock, watching Sun do whatever the hell it was Sun did? Because that's what she'd done all day yesterday—just stand there. Richard had gotten him up to speed on the farm's business and he'd spent some time haltering and walking the Percheron foals but he'd always been aware of the woman in the paddock.

She hadn't been watching him, which was a weird feeling. Women were always aware of what he was doing, waiting for their opportunity to strike up a conversation. He could make eye contact with a woman when he walked into a club and know that, six hours later, she'd be going back to his hotel with him. All he had to do was wait for the right time for her to make her move. She would come to him. Not the other way around.

But this horse trainer? He'd caught the way her hard glare had softened and she'd tilted her head when he'd complimented her little donkey. That was the kind of look a woman gave him when she was interested—when she was going to be in his bed later.

Not the kind of look a woman gave him when she proceeded to ignore him for the rest of the day. And night.

Phillip Beaumont was not used to being ignored. He was the life of the party. People not only paid attention to what he was doing, who he was doing it with, what he was wearing—hell, who he was tweeting about—but they paid good money to do all of that with him. It was his job, for God's sake. People always noticed him.

Except for her.

He should have been insulted yesterday. But he'd been so surprised by her attitude that he hadn't given a whole lot of thought to his wounded pride.

She was something else. A woman apart from others.

Variety is the spice of life, he thought as he strolled down to the barn. That had to be why he was so damned glad to see her and that donkey in the middle of the paddock again, Sun still doing laps around them both. But, Phillip noted, the horse was only trotting and making a few small bucks with his hind legs. Phillip wasn't sure he'd seen Sun this calm since…well, since Asia.

For a moment, he allowed himself to be hopeful. So three other trainers had failed. This Jo Spears might actually work. She might save his horse.

But then he had to go and ruin Sun's progress by saying, "Good morning."

At the sound of Phillip's voice, Sun lost it. He reared back, kicking his forelegs and whinnying with such terror that Phillip's hope immediately crumbled to dust. Betty looked at him and he swore the tiny thing rolled her eyes.

But almost immediately, Sun calmed down—or at least stopped making that God-awful noise and started running.

"You got that part right today," Jo said in that low voice of hers.

"It's good?" He looked her over—her legs spread shoulder-width apart, fingers hooked into her belt loops. Everything about her was relaxed but strong. He could imagine those legs and that backside riding high in the saddle.

And then, because he was Phillip Beaumont, he imagined those legs and that backside riding high in his bed.

Oh, yeah—it could be good. Might even be great.

"It's morning." She glanced over her shoulder at him and he saw the corner of her mouth curve up into a smile. "Yesterday when you said that, it was technically afternoon."

He couldn't help but grin at her. Boy, she was tough. When was the last time someone had tried to make him toe the line? Hell, when was the last time there'd even *been* a line?

And there was that smile. Okay, *half* a smile but still. Jo didn't strike him as the kind of woman who smiled at a man if she didn't actually want to. That smile told Phillip that she was interested in him. Or, at the very least, attracted to him. Wasn't that the same thing?

"Back at it again?"

She nodded.

Sun looped around the whole paddock, blowing past Phillip with a snort. His instinct was to step back from the fence, but he didn't want to project anything resembling fear—especially when she was actually inside the fence and he wasn't.

She pivoted, her eyes following the horse as he made another lap. Then, when he went back to running along the far side of the paddock again, she made that slow walk over to where Phillip stood.

Watching her walk was almost a holy experience. Instead of a practiced wiggle, Jo moved with a coiled grace that projected the same strength he'd felt in her handshake yesterday.

Did she give as good as she got? Obviously, in conversation the answer was *yes.* But did that apply to other areas?

She opened the gate and, Betty on her heels, walked out. When the gate closed behind her, she didn't come to him. She didn't even turn her head in his direction.

What would it take to get her to look at him? He could say something witty and crude. That would definitely get her attention. But instead of being scandalous and funny—which was how such comments went over when everyone was happily sloshed at a bar—he had a feeling that Jo might hit him for being an asshole.

Still, he was interested in that image of her riding him. He was the kind of man who was used to having female company every night. And he hadn't had any since he'd woken up at the farm.

He would enjoy spending time in Jo's company. He couldn't say why he liked the idea so much—she wouldn't make anything easy on him.

But that didn't bother him. In fact, he felt as if it was a personal challenge—one he was capable of meeting.

When was the last time he'd chased a woman? He tried to scroll through the jumbled memories but he wasn't coming up with anyone except...Suzie. Susanna Whaley, British socialite. She'd come from vulgar money—which was to say, by British definition, someone whose family had only gotten rich in the last century. She didn't care that Phillip was wealthy. She had enough money of her own. And she didn't care that he'd been famous. Before they'd met, she'd been dating some European prince. Phillip had been forced to work overtime just to get her phone number.

Something about that had been...well, it'd been *good*. He'd liked chasing her and she'd liked being chased. They'd dated internationally for almost a year. He'd looked at rings. He'd been twenty-six and convinced that *this* marriage would be different from his parents' marriage.

Then his father had died. Suzie had accompanied him to the funeral and met the entire Beaumont clan—his father's ex-wives, Phillip's half-siblings. All the bitter fighting and acrimonious drama that Phillip had tried so hard to get free of had been on full display. The police had gotten involved. Lawsuits had been filed.

So much for the Beaumont name.

The relationship had ended fairly quickly after that. He'd been upset, of course but deep down, he'd agreed with Suzie. His family—and, by extension, he himself—were too screwed up to have a shot at a happily-ever-after. They'd parted ways, she'd married that European prince and Phillip had gone right back to his womanizing ways. It was easier than thinking about what he'd almost had—and what he'd lost.

Still, he'd liked the chase. It'd been…different. Proof that it wasn't just his name or his money or even his famous face that a woman wanted. He'd had to prove his worth. That wasn't a bad thing.

Jo Spears clearly wasn't swayed by his name or his money. If she was as good a trainer as she claimed to be, she'd probably spent plenty of time in barns owned by equally rich, equally famous men and women. He didn't spend a lot of time with people who didn't want a piece of his name, his fortune—of him. The feeling was…odd.

He could stay out here for a few weeks. And he wouldn't mind having a little company.

He could chase Jo. It'd be fun.

"Coffee?" A thoughtful gesture was always a good place to begin.

She looked at the mugs in his hands and sniffed. "I don't drink."

He was going to have to switch brands of whiskey. Apparently Jack had a stronger smell than he remembered.

"Just coffee." When she gave him a look that could have peeled paint, he was forced to add, "In yours."

She took the mug, sniffed it several times and then took a tentative sip. "Thanks."

He stood there, feeling awkward, which was not normal. He wasn't awkward or unsure, not when it came to women. But every time he deployed one of his tried-and-true techniques on her, it backfired.

Oh yeah, this was going to be a challenge.

"How's it going?" he asked. Always good to focus on the basics.

That worked. She tilted her head in his direction, an appreciative smile on her face. "Not bad."

"I noticed," he continued, trying not to stare at that smile, "that you spend a lot of time standing in the paddock. With a donkey."

Her eyebrow curved up. "I do."

"Can I ask why, or are the mysteries of the horse whisperer secret?"

Damn, he lost her. Her warm smile went ice-cold in a heartbeat. "I do not *whisper*. I *train*."

Seducing her was going to prove harder than hell if he couldn't stop pissing her off. "Sensitive about that?"

Oh, that was a vicious look, one that let him know she'd loaded up both barrels and was about to open fire. "I'd explain my rules to you again, but what guarantee do I have that you'll remember them *this* time?"

Ouch. But he wasn't going to let her know how close to the quick she'd cut. He wouldn't back up in fear from his horse and he sure as hell wouldn't do it from a woman. He gave her his wicked smile, one that always worked. "I can be taught."

"I doubt it." Her posture changed. Instead of leaning toward him, she'd pulled away, her upper body angled in the direction of the barn.

Okay, he needed a different approach here, one that didn't leave his flank open to attack. Yesterday, when he hadn't remembered meeting her, she'd warmed up while he'd patted Betty. Time to put this theory to the test.

"Come here, girl," he said, crouching down and pulling the baggie of carrots out of his back pocket. "Do you like carrots?"

Betty came plodding over to him and snatched the carrot out of his hand. "That's a good girl."

"Did you bring one for Sun?"

"I did." He hadn't, but he'd brought enough. "But I don't think he likes me enough to let me give him one."

Then he looked up at her. Her light brown eyes were focused on his face with such intensity that it seemed she was seeing into him.

He fished another carrot out and looked at the horse that was still going in pointless circles around the paddock. Yeah, no getting close to *that* without getting trampled. "Like I said, I don't think he likes me."

"He doesn't *not* like you, though." She kept her gaze on the horse.

"How do you figure?" Betty snuffled at his hand, so he gave her the carrot he was holding. He still had two left. "Every time he sees me, he goes ballistic."

Jo sighed, which did some impressive things with her chest. "No, every time he sees you, it's something different. He doesn't like the different part. It has nothing to do with you. If you want to see what he does when he actively hates someone, you can call Richard out here."

"He hates Richard?" Although, now that he thought about it, Sun often did seem more agitated when the farm manager was around.

She nodded. "Richard and your hands are the ones who've shot him with the tranq gun, lassoed him in his stall and, from Sun's point of view, generally terrorized him. You don't have those negative associations in Sun's mind."

Everything she said made sense. He palmed another carrot, wondering if he should give it to the donkey or if he should try to walk into the paddock and give it to his horse. He'd be risking death, but it might be a positive thing the horse could associate with him. "He just doesn't like change?"

"Nope." She looked at his hand, then nodded to where there was a water bucket and a feed bucket hanging on the side of the paddock. "Put it in his bucket. But go slow."

"Okay." So it felt a little ridiculous to move at a snail's pace around the fence. But he noticed that Sun slowed to a trot and watched him.

Phillip held up the remaining two carrots so that Sun could see them and then dropped them over the fence and into the bucket. Then Phillip slowly worked his way back to where Jo was standing.

The approval on her face was something new. Something good. Wow, she could be pretty when she smiled.

"How was that?" He felt a little like a puppy begging for approval, but, for some reason, it was important to him.

Her smile deepened. "You *can* be taught."

"I'm a very quick study." He didn't walk over to her or run his hand down her arm—all things that worked wonders in a club—but he didn't need to. The blush that graced her cheeks was more than good enough to know that, no matter how icy or judgmental she could be, she was also a flesh-and-blood woman who responded to him.

Oh, yeah—the chase was *on*.

She looked away first. Aside from the blush and the smile, she gave no other sign of interest. She didn't lean in his direction, she didn't compliment him again. All she said was, "Watch," as she looked at Sun.

The horse was still trotting, but Phillip realized that each pass brought him closer to the buckets. Within a few minutes, he was making small loops back and forth right in front of the carrots.

He could probably smell them. Phillip hoped the horse would realize they were treats.

Sun slowed down enough that he was moving at a fast walk. He dipped his long nose into the bucket but before Phillip could allow himself to be hopeful, the horse knocked the whole thing off the fence, spilling the carrots and leftover grain on the ground. Then he was off again, running and bucking and throwing a hell of a fit.

"Damn."

"It's not you," Jo said again. "It's different. He's got to get used to someone leaving him a treat."

"And in the meantime?"

She shrugged. "We wait."

"Wait for what?"

"Wait for him to get tired."

He looked at her. "*This* is your grand plan to save him? Wait for him to get bored?" At his words, Sun began to rear up.

Jo sighed. "Don't you ever get tired?"

"Excuse me?"

"*Tired.*" She spoke the word carefully, as if she were pronouncing it for someone who didn't speak English. "Don't you get tired of the days and the nights blending together with no beginning and no end? Of waking up and not knowing who you are or where you are or most importantly of all, *what* you've done? Tired of realizing that you've done something horrible, something there's no good way to move on from, so you angle for that blackout again so you don't have to think about what you've become?"

She turned her face to him. Nothing about her was particularly lovely at this moment, but there was something in her eyes that wouldn't let him go.

"Doesn't it ever just wear you out?"

He did something he didn't usually allow himself to do—he glared at her. She couldn't know what she was talking about and, as far as he was concerned, she was not talking about him.

Still, her words cut into him like small, sharp knives and although it made no sense—she was wrong about him and that was *final*—he wanted to drink the rest of his coffee and let the whiskey in it take the edge off the inexplicable pain he felt, but she was watching him. Waiting to see if he'd buckle.

Well, she could just keep right on waiting. "I have no idea what you're talking about." His voice came out quieter than he'd meant it to. He almost sounded shaky to his own ears. He didn't like that. He didn't betray weakness, not to his family, not to anyone.

A shadow of sadness flickered across her face, but it was gone as she turned back to the paddock. "If that's what gets you through the night." She didn't wait for him to deny it. "Sun's been in this paddock for three straight days now. Sooner or later, he's going to get tired of doing the same thing over and over again. He'll want to do something different. Anything different, really, as long as it's not going mad. That's when I'll get him."

Going mad. Was that how she thought of the horse? Of him?

He needed to get the conversation onto firmer ground. Thus far, she'd responded best when he'd actively engaged her about horses and donkeys—not when the focus had been on him. "If he gets bored, won't he start cribbing or something? We've got collars that keep him from doing that, but I don't want to try and put one on him at this stage."

Cribbing happened when horses got bored. They bit down on the wood in their stalls or their rubber buckets and sucked in air. It seemed harmless at first, but it could lead to colic. And colic could be deadly.

Jo pivoted—not a sideways glance, but her whole body turned to him. He kept his eyes above her neck, and saw how she looked at him—confused, yes. But there was more to it than that.

"Really." The way she said it, it wasn't a question. More a wonderment.

He kept his voice casual. "You may not believe this, but I actually know a great deal about horses. My father had a racehorse back in 1987 that died of colic when the former farm manager hadn't realized the mare was cribbing. Yet another stumbling block in my father's eternal quest to win a Triple Crown."

That had been a bad year. Hardwick Beaumont had fired the entire staff at the farm and some of his employees at the Brewery and had been so unbearable to be around that he'd probably hastened his second divorce by at least two years.

Needless to say, it hadn't been much fun for Phillip. Even back then, the farm had been a sanctuary of sorts— a place to get away from half-siblings and step-parents. A place where Hardwick realized he *had* a second son, where they did things together. Even if those things were just leaning on a pasture fence and watching the trainers work the horses.

Hardwick had talked to Phillip during those times. Not Chadwick, not his new babies with his new wife. Just Phillip. The rest of the time, Hardwick had always been too busy running the Beaumont Brewery and having affairs to pay any attention to Phillip. But on the farm...

Phillip had cried that day. He'd cried for Maggie May, the horse who'd died, and he'd cried when the farm staff— the same grizzled old cowboys who'd always been happy to saddle up Phillip's pony and let him ride around the property—had been kicked out. Up until that day, he'd always thought the farm was a place safe from the real world, but all it had taken was one prize-winning mare's death to rip the veil from his eyes.

"Maggie May—that was the mare's name, right?"

Phillip snapped his attention back to the woman standing four feet from him. She was looking at Sun, who'd calmed down to an almost-mellow trot, but there was a sadness about her that, for once, didn't carry the weight of disappointment. It was almost as if she felt bad for the horse.

"You know about that?"

This time, she did give him the side-eye. "I'm also a quick study."

Electricity sparked between them. He felt it. She had to have felt it—why else did that pretty blush grace her cheeks again? "What else do you know about me?"

It was unusual to ask, more unusual to not know the answer. But she'd confounded him at every single turn thus far and, he realized, it was because she knew far more about him that he was anticipating.

She shrugged. "I always do my homework before I take a job. You're an easy man to find online."

But Maggie May—that horse wouldn't pop up in the first twenty pages of a web search. That sort of detail would be buried deep underneath an avalanche of Tumblr feeds and press releases. That was the sort of detail someone would really have to dig to come up with.

"Are you always this thorough, then?"

She didn't hesitate. "Always." Her blush deepened. "But how can I be sure that your reported horse sense is on the level?" She tried to give him a cutting look, but didn't quite make it.

So she was aware of the magnitude of his reputation. That certainly explained her disapproval of his high-flying lifestyle. But there was something underneath that, something deeper.

Something interested.

He recalled doing an interview in *Western Horseman*. He'd had a particularly bad month of headlines. Chadwick had been ready to kill him, so his half-brother Matthew had suggested setting up the interview to show people that there was more to Phillip Beaumont than just scandals.

The reporter had spent three days on the farm with Phillip, following him around as he evaluated his horses, worked with Richard, and generally projected a sane, in-control appearance. The write-up had been so well received that Chadwick had been almost charitable to him for months after that.

That had to be what she was talking about. She'd probably assumed that one main article about him being a real cowboy was a PR plant. And she hadn't been half wrong.

Except he was a real cowboy—at least, he was when he was on the farm. This was the only place where he fit—where he could be Phillip instead of Hardwick's forgotten second son. The horses never cared who he was. They just cared that he was a good man who looked out for them.

Was that what she needed—to know that the horses came first for him? "I guess I'll have to prove myself to you."

"I guess you will," she agreed.

Oh, yeah—the chase was *on*. Jo was unlike any woman he'd ever pursued before. Instead of being a turn-off, he was more and more intrigued by her. She refused to cut him a single bit of slack, but all the signals were there.

Maybe she was a good girl who was intrigued by his bad boy antics. Maybe she'd like a little walk on the wild side. But the things that got her attention weren't the bad boy things. She noticed his interactions with the horses more.

Bad boy with a healthy dash of cowboy—*that* was something he could pull off. If she needed to know that his horse sense, as she called it, was on the level, then he'd have no problem showing her exactly how much he really understood about horses.

Starting now. "I need to get to the foals," he said, leaning toward her just a tad. She didn't pull back. "I'll stop by later and see if Sun ate his carrots."

She did not turn those pretty eyes in his direction, but her grin was broad enough that he knew he'd said the right thing. "I'd like that," she said in a low voice. Then she seemed to remember herself. Her cheeks shot bright red. "I mean, that'd be good. For Sun." Then, before he could say anything else, she opened the gate and walked into the paddock, the tiny donkey at her heels.

Interesting. She might try to act as if she were a tough-as-nails woman, but underneath was someone softer—someone who was enjoying the chase.

Oh, yeah—it'd be good, all right.

Might even be great.

Four

What the hell was she doing?

Jo stood in the middle of the paddock as Sun wore down. At least he was finally wearing down after three days. He kept looping closer to where the carrots lay in the dirt near his bucket.

The horse was calming down, but Jo? She was beginning to spiral out of control.

She had absolutely no business flirting with Phillip Beaumont. None. The list of reasons why started and ended with whiskey. And vodka. And tequila. She'd always been partial to tequila—she thought. She couldn't really remember.

And that was exactly why she had no business encouraging him. *Really, Jo? Really? It'd be good if he stopped by later?*

She didn't want to look forward to seeing him again. She was not the least bit curious to know if he'd bring her more coffee or Betty and Sun some carrots. She didn't even want to know what he was doing with the Percheron foals.

She was not here for Phillip Beaumont.

Now if she could get that through her thick skull.

It was hard, though. No one brought her coffee. Everyone took her at her word when she said she didn't hook up and left her alone. Which was how she liked it.

Well, maybe she didn't like it. It was a lonely life, never letting herself get close to people.

She'd made friends with Whitney Maddox last winter because Whitney...understood. Whitney had been down the same path, after all. It was easy to be friends with someone else who only trusted animals.

But Phillip? Not only did he *not* leave her alone, he kept coming back for more. It was almost as if he enjoyed her refusal to kowtow to him.

She started to wonder why that was but stopped. She didn't care if he thought she was a hoot or a breath of fresh air or if he was silently mocking her every single move. She *didn't* care.

Not much, anyway.

She rubbed Betty's ears and focused on Sun. Her thoughts didn't often get away from her like this, not anymore. And when they did...

No. She wasn't going to have a bad night. She wasn't even going to have a bad day. She forced herself to breathe regularly. Just because Phillip Beaumont was handsome and tempting and got this smile on his face when he looked at her....

Right. Not happening.

His reputation preceded him. He probably looked at every woman as if she were the one person he'd been waiting for. This had nothing to do with her and everything to do with the fact that she was the only woman on the ranch.

She knew all these things. The sheer logic of the situation should have defused her baser instincts. That's how it'd always worked before.

So why was she thinking about that smile? Or the way his hands would feel on her body? Or what his body would feel like against hers?

Jesus, this was getting out of control. She'd left men in her past with the tequila and the nights she couldn't remember. She would not be tempted by a man who was every one of her triggers wearing a pair of work jeans.

Work jeans that fit him really well.

Damn.

Betty leaned against her, anchoring Jo to reality. She let herself rub the back of her neck, her fingers tracing the scar tissue that she'd earned the hard way. This was not the first time she'd been tempted by a man. The first job she'd taken off her parents' ranch had featured a hot young cowboy named Cade who liked to raise hell on a Friday night. Yes, it'd been a year since the accident at that point, but Jo had healed. She'd been flattered to know that she hadn't managed to totally destroy her looks and, truthfully, she *had* been tempted.

Cade had been her idea of a good time for years. It would have been so easy to take him up on his offer for a little fun. So damned easy to get into his truck, not knowing where they were going and not knowing if she'd remember it in the morning.

But she was tired of not remembering. So she'd passed on Cade's offer and never forgotten him. Funny how that worked out.

Sun was calmer today. That was good. The carrots had provided him something to focus on.

Finally, after Jo spent an hour and a half trying not to think about Phillip's smile or his jeans while she waited for Sun to get tired, the horse slowed down to what looked like an angry walk, as if he'd only stopped running as a favor to her. He continued to pace near the carrots.

Jo waited. Would the horse actually eat one? That would be making more progress than she'd hoped for. And if Sun improved faster, the sooner she could pack up Betty into the trailer and be on her way to the next job, far away from the temptation named Phillip Beaumont.

Sun dipped his nose into the water bucket and took a couple of deep drinks, then leaned down to sniff the carrots.

And pawed them into mush.

Close, she thought with a weary sigh.

She tried to focus on the positive here. Sun was, in fact, getting bored with being out-of-control. Something as innocent as carrots hadn't sent him into spasms of panic. He hadn't even destroyed them outright. He'd been curious—so much so that his curiosity had distracted him from his regularly scheduled pacing. This was all good news.

She heard hoofbeats coming up the drive. Sun heard them too and, with a whinny that sounded closer to a horse than a demon, resumed trotting and kicking.

Moving slowly, Jo turned to see a beautiful pair of Percherons hitched to a wagon loaded with hay and driven by none other than Phillip Beaumont, who was sitting high on a narrow bench. His coffee mug was nowhere in sight. The wagon looked as though it was a hundred years old—wooden wheels painted red and gray. The whole thing was a scaled down version of the Beaumont Beer wagon that the Percherons pulled in parades and commercials.

Phillip put both reins in one hand and honest-to-God tipped his hat to her. Heat flushed her face.

"Did he eat the carrots?"

"He pulverized them." She pointed to the orange-colored dirt.

"Damn." He looked a little disappointed, but not as if the world had ended. "I'll try again tomorrow."

He seemed so sincere about it—a man who was concerned about his horse.

She'd be lying if she said she didn't find it endearing. "That'd be good."

She was pretty sure this was flirting. Maybe she was being the ridiculous one, reading intent where there was none.

Her face got hotter.

"I can't help but notice," Phillip went on as if she weren't slowly turning into a tomato, "that you've spent at least two days standing in the middle of a paddock."

"This is true."

He jiggled the reins. "There's more to this farm than just that patch of dirt." The invitation sounded pretty casual, but then he turned that smile in her direction. That was a smile that promised all kinds of wicked fun. "Want to go for a ride?"

That was flirting. It had to be.

And she had no idea how to respond.

After a moment's pause, Phillip went on. "I'm getting Marge and Homer here used to pulling the wagon. I'm headed out to the other side of the ranch, where I keep the Appaloosas. Have you seen them?"

"No." She hadn't even really seen the Percherons—but she wanted to. Could she accept this ride at face value—a chance to see the rest of the storied Beaumont Farm and the collection of horses it contained? "You named your horses after *The Simpsons?*"

"Doesn't everyone?" Good lord, that grin was going to be her undoing. "I'd love to get your professional opinion on them and the Appaloosas."

There—now did that qualify as flirting or not? Dang it, she was *so* out of practice.

He must have sensed her hesitation. "I'm just going to drop off the hay. Twenty, thirty minutes tops."

Wait—a multi-millionaire like Phillip Beaumont moved his own hay? This she had to see for herself. "One condition—I want to drive."

For a moment, the good-time grin on his face cracked, but she was serious. Drunk driving—whether it was a team of Percherons or a Porsche—was a non-starter for her.

Then the grin was back. "Can you handle a team?" His voice had dropped a notch and was in danger of smoldering. If she hadn't seen the crack in his mask before, she might not have noticed it this time. He hid it well.

"I can see how you'd question my skills, what with me being an equestrian professional." He notched an eyebrow at her and she almost felt bad for being a smart-ass. So she added, "I was raised on a ranch. I can drive a team."

"Ever driven Percherons?"

"There's a first for everything."

That was flirting—for her, anyway. Phillip took it that way, too. "Then come on."

He waited while she exited the paddock, her donkey on her heels. "What about Betty?" she asked after she got the gate closed.

She couldn't leave Betty alone with Sun. But she didn't want Betty wandering around the farm. She was small enough that, if she really put her mind to it, she could fall down a hole or get stuck in a gap in the fences.

"I thought she might like to try out a new pasture, meet some of the not-crazy horses we have here," he replied, pointing to a gate about two hundred yards up the drive. Clearly, he'd been anticipating this question. There was a certain measure of thoughtfulness about him that was, she had to admit, appealing. "The grass is always greener on the other side."

She grinned up at him. "So it is. I'll follow the wagon up."

She gave Sun a final look. The horse was actually standing still, watching them with the kind of look that seemed to say that he was taking in everything they did and said. Would he freak out as they left him alone or would he watch them go?

Phillip gave her one of those old-fashioned nods of his head and clucked to his team. The wagon started and she followed, Betty on her heels.

This was just some professional consideration, right? Phillip was a noted horseman and she was an increasingly noted horse trainer. His asking her to look at other horses on the farm had nothing to do with any real or imagined interest on his part and everything to do with getting the most out of what he was paying her.

When they got to the gate at the pasture across the road, Phillip surprised her again by hopping down off the wagon and opening the gate for Betty. "There you go, girl. Enjoy the grass—we'll be back."

Betty gave him one of her looks as she plodded past him into the pasture. Phillip latched the gate behind her. "Have fun!" He turned to Jo, the goofiest grin she'd ever seen on his face.

"What?"

"I like Betty. Everything about her is hilarious. Here, let me help you."

Now, Jo was perfectly capable of climbing up onto the narrow seat of a rack wagon all by herself, but Phillip moved to her side and placed a hand on the small of her back. "Just step up on the wheel there...."

His touch sent licking flames of heat up and down her back. His hand was strong and confident against her. How long had it been since a man had touched her? Since...

Bad. Bad, bad, *bad*. She slammed the breaks on that line of thinking and shook him off before she did something insane like pretend to stumble so he'd be forced to catch her. "I have done this before, you know."

She didn't catch the double entendre until he said, "Have you, now?" low and close to her ear. His breath was warm and didn't smell like whiskey.

It had been a long time. Really long. Could she indulge herself, just this once, and not slide back down to rock bottom? She had needs. It'd be nice to have someone else help her meet them.

She looked over her shoulder at Phillip, who was less than two feet away, an expectant look on his face. But he didn't press the issue or find some excuse to keep touching her. He just waited for her response.

She swallowed and hefted herself into the seat. This was starting to look like a bad idea—all of it. She tried to refocus her thinking. She was at the Beaumont Farms because this job would make her reputation as a trainer. Phillip Beaumont was not just an attractive, attentive man with a reputation as one of the better lovers in the world, he was the client who'd hired her to save his horse.

And getting in the wagon to see the farm and his other horses was…was…a wise business decision. He might have another horse who needed retraining, which would mean more money for her, a better reference.

That was a stretch and she knew it, especially when Phillip swung up into the seat and managed to make it look smooth. He settled onto the bench next to her, their thighs touching, and handed her the reins. "Marge likes to go fast, Homer likes to go slow. Try to keep them together." Then he leaned back, slung one arm behind her on the bench and said, "Show me what you can do."

He wasn't touching her but she swore she could feel the heat from his arm anyway. She gathered the reins and flicked them. "Up!"

Phillip chuckled as the horses began to walk. "Up?"

"It's what we said at home. And," she couldn't help but point out, "it worked. What do you say?"

"I'm partial to 'Let's Go.' So you were raised on a ranch?"

She adjusted the reins in her hands until she had more tension on Marge's. "Yup." She felt as if she should say more, but small talk was not one of her strengths. Never had been. Maybe that's why parties had always been easier with a beer in her hand.

"Where's home?"

"Middle of nowhere, South Dakota. Nothing to do but stare at the grass."

"Oh? So you've been training horses your whole life?"

She shrugged. She didn't like talking about herself. She especially didn't like talking about the six or so years that were a total blur. So she skipped it entirely.

"Not like this. But I'd come back to the ranch after college—" That was the most diplomatic way to put it. "—and a neighbor's barn caught fire. He lost four horses, but one survived. Oaty was his name. That horse was a mess. The vet almost put him down twice but..."

"But you couldn't let him do that." Phillip's tone was more than sympathetic. He understood.

"Nope. I just watched him. For days. And the longer I watched him, the more I could understand him. He was terrified and I couldn't blame him."

"You waited for him to get bored?"

"More like to calm down. Took about a month before I could get close enough to brush him. He was scarred and his coat never did grow back right on his flank, but he's still out on my parents' ranch, munching grass and hanging out with the donkeys."

The day she'd saddled old Oaty up and ridden him across the ranch had been one of the best days of her life. For so long she'd felt lost and confused and hadn't known why, but saving Oaty had been saving herself. She hadn't given up on Oaty and she wouldn't give up on herself.

She was good at something—saving horses no one else could. She'd stayed on her parents' ranch for a few more years, driving around the state to other semi-local ranches to work with their horses, and as her successes had mounted, so had the demand for her services.

Besides, a woman could only live with her parents for so long. So she'd bought her trailer and hit the road, Betty in tow, determined to make a name for herself. It'd taken years, but she'd finally made it to a place like Beaumont Farms—the kind of place where money was no object.

"That must have been huge for you."

"Oaty was a tough case. Probably the toughest I've had up until now."

Phillip chuckled. "I'm honored to be the toughest case."

She couldn't help it. She turned to look at him. "It's not really an honor."

Their gazes met. There was something raw in his eyes, something…honest.

She did not fix people. She did not sleep with people. She didn't do anything involving alcohol anymore. She'd been clean and sober for ten years and had never crossed back over to the dark side. Apart from a long-ago cowboy named Cade, she'd never once been tempted by a man.

Until now.

She shouldn't be attracted to Phillip and most certainly not interested in him.

But she was. Against all known logic and common sense, she was.

"Here," she said, thrusting the reins at him. "You drive."

Five

"You really haul your own hay?" Jo asked as she watched him grab a bale.

The question struck him as funny, considering the woman was holding a bale at mid-chest without breaking a sweat.

"Of course. This is a working farm, after all."

"But *you* work?"

He shot her a smarmy look, but it felt differently on his face than it normally did. He picked up a bale, aware of how she was looking at his arms. "I work." Then he flexed.

She could be quite lovely when she blushed—as she was doing right now. She wasn't a traditionally beautiful woman, what with her strong jaw, dark hair that brushed her shoulders and her flannel shirt with only one button undone, but underneath that...

She wasn't his type. But he was having trouble remembering what he liked so much about all the women he normally kept company with. Compared to Jo, they all looked…the same.

"This way," he said, leading her back to the hay room.

Working in silence, they got the hay unloaded in a matter of minutes. He carried in the final bale and turned to get out of her way. But he didn't walk back out to the wagon. He stood there for a moment in the dim room, watching her heft her final bale on top of his. Then she turned and caught him staring at her.

A ripple of tension moved across her shoulders and he thought she was going to blow past him and rush for the open air. After all, they could do things in this hay room and no one would be the wiser. But she'd made her position pretty damned clear. If she stormed out of here, he wouldn't be the least bit surprised.

She didn't. Instead, she hooked her thumbs in her belt, leaned back against the hay bales and looked at him as if she was waiting for him to make his move. No overt come-on, no suggestive posturing. Just standing there, watching him watch her.

He knew what he wanted to do. He wanted to press her back against the bale and find out if she liked things soft and sweet and pretty like her blush or if she wanted it rough and tough.

But, as she stood there and waited, he *didn't* want to. Which didn't make any sense. Of course he wanted to kiss her, to touch her. But…

Something stopped him.

She was starting to unnerve him. Suddenly, he realized this must be what his horse felt like. She could stand here all day and wait for him to get bored.

So he did something. Something that bordered on being out of character for him. He did not ask her to dinner and he did not ask her if she'd like to soak in his hot tub with a view. "Would you like to see the Appaloosas?"

The corner of her mouth moved up into what might have been a pleased smile on someone else. It was almost as if that had been the thing she'd hoped he'd say. It was weird how good that little half-smile of approval made him feel. "I would."

He walked her through the barn to the nearby pasture where his Appaloosas were grazing. "I've got four breeding mares," he told her, pointing the spotted horses out to her. "We usually get two foals a year out of them. We have between six and nine on site at any given time."

"What do you do with them?"

"Sell them. They're good workhorses, but I sell a lot to Hollywood. I focus on the blanket-with-spots coloring, which is what producers want." He pointed to the nearest mare. "See? Black in the front, white flank with spots in the back."

She gave him that look again, the one that said he was making a fool of himself. "I know what a blanket Appaloosa is, you know."

He grinned at her. She did *not* cut him any slack. Why did he like it so much? "Sorry. The women I normally hang out with don't know much about horses."

"I'm not like other women."

He couldn't help it. He leaned toward where she was, his voice dropping an octave. "A fact I've become more aware of every day."

She let him wait a whole minute before she acknowledged what he'd said. "Are you hitting on me?"

"No." Even though she wasn't looking at him, he still saw the way her face twisted in disagreement, so he added, "By all agreed-upon Dude Law, this barely breaks the threshold for flirting."

She snorted in what he hoped was amusement. "Do you have an Appaloosa stallion?"

"No. I use different stock to keep the genetics clean."

"Smart," she said in the kind of voice that made it clear she hadn't expected a smart answer.

"I told you, I know a great deal about horses." He pointed out the yearling. "That's Snowflake. I've got a breeder who's interested in him out in New York if his coat fills in right."

"Why do you breed them?"

"I like them. They've got history. The story is that my great-grandfather, Phillipe Beaumont, drove a team of Percherons he'd brought over from France across the Great Plains after the Civil War and then traded one with the Nez Perce for one of their Appaloosas—he considered that a fair trade."

She looked at him again, those soft hazel eyes almost level with his. If this were any other woman in the world, he'd touch her. He was thinking about doing it anyway, but he didn't want to push his luck.

He'd basically promised that they were just here to look at the horses, so that's all they were going to do. He'd given his word. He wanted the woman, but he wanted her to want him, too.

And she just might, given the way she was looking at him, her full lips slightly parted and her head tilted to one side as if she really wouldn't mind a kiss. "You keep Appaloosas because your great-grandfather bought one a hundred and fifty years ago?"

"More like a hundred and thirty years. Of course, he only got the one Appaloosa, so my mares don't go back that far. But the Percherons do."

Man, he could get lost in her eyes. He could only guess at what she was thinking right now.

Because she didn't seem to be thinking about horses. "You spend a lot of time out here with them?"

"Always have. The farm is a more pleasant place to be than the Beaumont Mansion."

That was the understatement of the year. Growing up a Beaumont in the shadow of Hardwick's chosen son, Chadwick, had been an experience in privileged neglect. No one had paid a bit of attention to Phillip. His mother had divorced his father when he was five, but Hardwick had retained full custody of the boys for reasons that, as far as Phillip could tell, could only be called spiteful.

Hardwick had devoted all of his attention to Chadwick, grooming him to run the Beaumont Brewery. Phillip?

No one had cared. When his mother had lost the lengthy custody battles, she acted as if Phillip had purposefully chosen Hardwick just to punish her. Then Hardwick had gotten married again—and again, and again—and always paid more attention to his new wife and his new children. Because there were always new wives and new children.

Phillip had been all but invisible in his own home. He could come and go and do as he pleased and it just didn't matter. The freedom was heady. What had grades mattered to him? They hadn't. Teachers didn't dare make him toe the line because of his father's reputation. He'd discovered that, although no one cared a bit for him at home, people out in the world cared about his name a great deal—so much so that he could break every rule in the book and no one would stop him.

By the time he'd gotten to college, he had his pick of women. He had a well-deserved reputation as a man who would satisfy. Women were complicated. They liked to feel sexy and desirable and wanted. Most of them wanted to feel swept away, but some liked to call the shots. He'd learned that early.

Not much had changed since then. His reputation always preceded him. Women came to him, not the other way around. And his brother Chadwick only cared what he did when he thought Phillip had made a spectacle of the Beaumont name. Chadwick was the only person who ever tried to make Phillip toe the line, and Phillip made him pay for it.

No one stopped Phillip Beaumont. Except possibly a horse trainer named Jo Spears.

"That surprises me," she said in her quiet tone. "You seem more like a big-city kind of man."

That's what she said. What he heard was 'party guy.' And he couldn't blame her. Beaumont Farms wasn't exactly the social center of the world.

"The big city has its advantages, it's true. But sometimes it's good to take a break from the hustle and bustle and slow down."

He'd always come out to the farm to get away from the tension that was his family. Here, there were rules. If he wanted to ride his pony, he had to brush that pony and clean the stall. If he wanted to drive the team with a wagon, he had to learn how to hook up the harness. And if he wanted to gentle the foals and get them used to being haltered, he had to be able to hold on to a rearing animal.

When he'd been a kid, this had been the only place in his life where there were consequences for his actions. If he screwed up or only half-assed something, then he fell off the horse because the girth wasn't tight enough or got kicked for startling a horse from behind.

But it'd also been the place where he'd done things right and gotten rewarded for it. When he got his pony saddled all by himself, he'd gotten to go for a ride with his father. When he'd learned how to walk around horses without scaring them, he'd gotten to spend more time working with them. And when he learned how to ask a horse to do something the right way, he'd gotten to race and jump and have a hell of a good time.

He'd gotten the attention of his father. Hardwick Beaumont had been a horseman through and through. It came with the Beaumont name and Hardwick had lived up to it.

His horse obsessions had followed all the usual paths—expensive Thoroughbred horses in an attempt to win the Triple Crown, lavish show horses designed to win gold and the Percherons, of course.

Phillip had been too big to be a jockey, so he couldn't ride for the Crown. He'd been a good rider, but never great. But he could talk horses and help with the Percherons. When it'd been just the two of them out on the farm, his father had not only noticed him, but approved of him. He'd never won the Triple Crown, but his jockeys and trainers had won the Preakness three times and Churchill Downs twice.

Horses had been the only thing that had set Phillip apart from Chadwick. Phillip was good with horses. He understood the consequences—never understood it better than when Maggie May had died. Horses were valuable and, as the second son, it was his duty to keep that part of the Beaumont legacy alive.

The only time he missed his father was when he was on the farm.

"So, you work," Jo repeated, calling him back to himself.

She wasn't looking at him, but he felt as if he had her full attention. "Yes."

"Do you clean tack?"

The question would have been odd coming from any other woman. Somehow, he wasn't surprised she'd asked it. "I have on occasion."

He could only see half her face, but he didn't miss the quick smile. "Can you be in the paddock around eight tomorrow morning?" Then she angled her face in his direction. "Or is that too early for you?"

Hell, yeah it was early. But he wasn't going to let her know that. "I'll bring the coffee." Doubt—he recognized it now—flashed over her face. "You take yours black, right?"

She held his gaze for another long moment. Finally, she said, "Yup," and let it drop.

"You want to drive the team back to the barn?"

She brightened. "They're beautiful animals. I've never worked with them before."

He felt himself relax. He could talk horses, after all. As long as they came back to the horses, she wouldn't look at him as if she was disappointed in him. "Well, you've come to the right place. Have you seen any of the foals?"

Her eyes lit up. She really was striking. So very tough but underneath that… "Foals?" Then she sighed. "I need to get back to Sun."

"Maybe tomorrow afternoon?"

She dropped her chin and looked up at him through thick lashes. "I guess that depends on how well you clean tack."

There was that challenge again, writ large in both words and actions. Everything about her was a bet—one that he wanted to take. "I guess it does."

He could prove himself in the morning cleaning tack. It didn't matter why. He would show her that he knew his stuff and that he was good with his hands.

And then? He'd get out his carriage, the one with the roomy padded seat and the bonnet that provided a modicum of privacy. It was a big farm. Plenty of shady lanes hidden behind old-growth trees where a couple could have a picnic in private.

She was a challenge, all right. But he'd bet that he could win her over, even if he had to clean tack to do it.

Six

Phillip strolled up to the paddock at 7:58, two mugs in hand. "Good morning," he called out. "What are you doing?"

"Waiting for you," she replied, setting the cutter saddle down on the blanket she'd laid out in the middle of the paddock. Betty was nibbling the untrampled grass near the gate, but she looked up as Phillip approached and went to meet him.

Behind Jo, Sun whinnied. She turned in time to see him trot past his buckets. Checking for carrots? That was a good sign.

"I'm on time *and* under budget." His tone—light and teasing and promising good things—made her look up. Even though the dawning light of morning was just casting the farm in pinks and yellows, Phillip's smile was warm and bright. He reached through the gate to rub Betty's little head. "I even brought carrots."

Oh. He'd shaved today. The four-day growth he'd been

working on was gone and suddenly he looked more like the man in the commercials—the one to whom women flocked.

No flocking. She would not flock. This exercise in tack was not about spending time with Phillip Beaumont. This was about the fact that Phillip was Sun's owner. She was just encouraging the relationship between the horse and the man.

"Grab the saddle," she said, nodding toward the Trilogy English jumping saddle she'd set on top of the fence. The cutter saddle was by far the more complicated of the two saddles. Cleaning it would take her hours. If Phillip knew what he was doing, the jumping saddle would take him forty-five minutes. An hour, tops. And if he didn't know what he was doing...

Why did she want him to be able to clean a saddle so badly? It was just tack. True, both saddles were high-end. She felt bad about using them, but there hadn't been a lower-end option. She took some comfort in the fact that this wouldn't be a hardship for someone with the Beaumont name.

Phillip's brows jumped up. "And?"

"And open the gate, walk in slowly, and have a seat." She motioned to the blanket on the ground.

"What about the carrots?"

"Hang on to them. We might need them later."

"Okay." He grabbed the saddle and opened the gate.

Sun stopped trotting, stood still and watched Phillip—at least, until the gate was latched. Then he went into a round of bucking that would have won him first prize at any rodeo.

Phillip froze, just two steps inside the fence. Jo turned to watch Sun throw his fit. He'd been calming down for her quite nicely, but she couldn't say this was a surprise.

He didn't like change and another person in the paddock was a big change. Even if it was the person with the carrots.

"Should I leave?" Phillip asked. She had to admire the fact that he didn't sound as though he was quaking in his boots. If he could keep calm, Sun would chill out faster.

"Nope. Just walk toward me. Slowly."

She kept her eyes on Sun as Phillip made the long walk. Sun wasn't bucking as high as he had during the first days and he certainly wasn't working himself into a lather.

Phillip made it to the blanket, handed her a thermal mug and set the saddle down at his feet. Betty sniffed the saddle while Jo sniffed the coffee. "Thanks." Black, with no secret ingredients. Had he spiked his coffee again this morning? If so, he'd gone light. She didn't catch a hint of whiskey about him.

Instead, he smelled like…she leaned closer. Bay rum spice, warm and clean and tempting.

When he said, "Now what?" she almost jumped out of her skin.

Right. She had a job here, one that required her full attention. They couldn't sit down while Sun was bucking. The risk that he might charge was too great. But she was going to stop standing in this paddock today, by God. She could feel it. "We wait. Welcome to standing."

So they stood. Betty wandered back over to where the grass was greener, completely unconcerned with either Sun's antics or what the people were doing.

How long could Phillip do this? Thus far, he had not struck her as a man of inaction. Which was admirable, but there was something to be said for just watching. She was thinking he'd only last about five minutes before he started to get twitchy. Seven at the most.

After about ten minutes, Phillip asked, "How long is this going to take?"

She tried not to smile. *Not bad.* "As long as it takes."

Another five minutes passed. "Maybe I should give him the carrots? Would that help?"

"Nope."

"Why not?" Phillip was starting to sound exasperated. She wondered which one would crack first—the horse or the man.

"Because," she explained, "if you give him the carrots now, he'll associate carrots with temper tantrums. Wait until he's managed to be calm for at least ten minutes."

"Oh. Right."

They were silent for another five minutes as Sun continued to go through the motions.

"We're really just going to stand here?"

She couldn't help giving him a look. "Do you have a problem with silence?"

"No," he defended a little quicker than was necessary. Which was almost the same as a yes. "This just seems pointless."

This was not going how she'd thought it would. Yesterday, he'd seemed like a man who would understand what it took to retrain a horse. "Do you have something else you'd rather do than train your multi-million-dollar horse?"

That made him look a little more sheepish, which had the unfortunate side effect of making him look positively adorable. "No."

Sun reared up, which drew their attention. "See? He's a smart horse," she told Phillip. "He's picking up on your impatience. Just *be*, okay?"

"Okay."

She didn't think he could do it. Hell, the only reason she could do it was because she'd been in traction for a few months, physically incapable of doing anything but be still and quiet and painfully aware of her surroundings.

Months in traction, then almost another year out on her parents' ranch just sitting around while her body healed, watching the world. God, she'd been so bored in the beginning. She'd hurt and couldn't take any of the good painkillers and none of the nurses would bring her a beer. She'd tried watching television, but that had only made things worse.

Then her granny, Lina Throws Spears, had come to sit with her. Sometimes, Lina had told her old Lakota stories about trickster coyotes and spiders, but most of the time she'd just sat, looking out the window at the parking lot.

It'd almost driven Jo insane. Lina had always been weird, burning sage and drinking tea. But then Jo had started to actually see the world around her. People came with balloons and hopeful smiles for new babies. People left with tissues in their hands and tears in their eyes when someone died. They fought and sometimes met for quickies in the back of the parking lot. Some smoked. Some drank. Some talked on cell phones.

They did things for reasons. And, if you paid attention, those reasons weren't that hard to figure out.

When she'd finally been discharged and went home, she hadn't been good for much. So she sat on her parents' porch and watched the ranch.

It'd always been such a boring place—or so she'd thought. But then she'd actually sat still and paid attention.

She'd noticed things that she'd never seen before, like the snake that lived under the porch and the starlings that lived in the barn. The barn cat napped in the sun until the sun moved and then he went mousing.

There'd been something peaceful about it. She watched the wind blow through the pastures and storms blow in. She watched her dad saddle the horses and her mom bake pies.

The world had felt…okay. She'd felt okay in it. She'd never been able to say that before. And then, when Oaty had survived that fire, she'd watched him and figured out what he'd been trying to say.

But getting to the point where she could understand a horse as messed up as Oaty had taken her well over a year. It was ridiculous to think that a man like Phillip Beaumont—known for his wild ways—would be able to just stand here and pay attention because she asked him to half an hour ago.

And he couldn't. He was trying, that she could see, but within fifteen minutes, his fingers were tapping against his legs, beating out a staccato rhythm of impatience.

Not surprisingly, Sun picked up on this. His hoofbeats against the ground nearly matched Phillip's rhythm.

"Stop," she said, reaching over and pulling his hand away from his leg.

Which meant she was now holding his hand.

His fingers wrapped around hers. "Sorry." He didn't sound particularly sorry.

She stood *very* still. Aside from handshakes, she hadn't touched a man in so long. The feeling of something as simple as holding hands was...

It was a lot. Heat bloomed from where his skin touched hers, which set off a chain reaction across her body. Her nipples tightened. They went hard in a way she'd forgotten about. Her heart rate picked up and she knew she was blushing but she couldn't help it.

Skin on skin. It was only a light touch, but for the first time in a very long time, desire coursed through her.

Oh, no—this was bad.

She couldn't pull her hand away. The sensations flooding her body—the weight growing heavy between her legs, the heat clouding her thinking—left her unable to do anything but stand there and *keep* touching him.

As she spun out of control, both Phillip and Sun seemed

to be calming down. Instead of drumming his fingers against his leg, he went to…

To rubbing his thumb against her skin.

Jo's head swam as desire hit her hard. One of the most attractive, wealthy, available men in the country was stroking the back of her hand.

Once, it'd taken far less than this—coffee in the morning, horses in the afternoon, a light touch—to get her back to a room. Or into a car. Or even just up against a wall. Once, all a guy would have had to do was buy her a drink and maybe tell her she was hot. *Maybe.* That'd been all the reason she needed to go off with another man she didn't know, to wake up in a place she couldn't remember.

How was Phillip doing this to her? He hadn't pinned her against a wall or bitten her in that space between her neck and her shoulder or anything. He was just holding her hand! It shouldn't make her think of being pinned against walls and being bitten or touched. It just shouldn't.

In her confusion, she made the mistake of looking at him. He turned his head at almost the same time and smiled. That was it. Nothing but a nice, sexy, hot smile. For her.

Ten long years of no touching and no smiling caught up to Jo in milliseconds. She *wanted* him to pin her against the wall and bite that place on her neck. And a few other things. She wanted to feel his hands on a whole bunch of places. She wanted to know exactly how good this cowboy was.

This—this was exactly why she'd abstained from men. Something as small as a single touch having this much effect on her—it was like an alcoholic saying he could have one sip and be just fine.

Men, like drinking, were an all-or-nothing proposition for her. That's just the way it was. She was not going to fall off the wagon because Phillip Beaumont was gorgeous, thoughtful, rich and worried about his horse. She'd worked too hard to be the person she was now.

The look in his eyes got deeper. *Warmer*. And damn it all if it didn't make him look even hotter.

He was close enough that Jo could lean forward and kiss him.

Thank God, Sun saved her. He came to a halt in front of them, clearly trying to figure out what new thing the humans were doing.

Which made Phillip turn those beautiful eyes away from her. "Hey," he said in a quiet, strong voice that sent shivers racing down the back of her neck. "He stopped."

What's more than that, the horse didn't start back up when Phillip spoke. He just stood there. Then he *walked* over to where the buckets were. He stuck his nose into the food bucket and then looked back at Phillip. It was an amazing development.

"He wants a carrot," she told Phillip.

"Should I give him one?"

"Go ahead and put one in the bucket, but make sure he sees you've got more. After all, he did calm down and ask politely. He's earned a reward."

At this observation, Phillip turned a dazzling smile in her direction. "Do I get a reward, too?" he said in that same strong voice as the pad of his thumb moved over her hand again.

This time, the shivers were stronger.

His mouth settled from the dazzling smile into the grin that was so wicked she couldn't help but think about him scraping his teeth against her bare flesh as he pulled the snaps of her shirt apart....

"No," she gritted out, hoping she didn't sound as if she was about to start swooning.

She wasn't fooling him. She wasn't even fooling herself. He leaned forward, the air between them crystalizing into something so sharp it almost cut her. His grip on her hand tightened as he tried to pull her toward him. "Why not? I calmed down. I asked politely."

"You didn't do it on your own." She was desperate to stop touching him and completely unable to do so. "You have to earn a reward."

"And how do I do that?" Somehow, he managed to make it sound innocent and sensual all at the same time.

"Carrots for the horse. Then tack. Done right."

She jerked her hand out of his grasp, desperate.

He leaned forward, the air between them growing hot. He was going to kiss her and she was going to let him and if that happened, would she be able to control herself? Or would she be gone? Again?

His gaze searched hers. God, she probably looked like a deer in the headlights—blinded by his sheer sex appeal.

"One condition—I get to choose my own reward." His voice dropped to a dangerous level—silky and sensual and promising all sorts of good things. "I don't like carrots." Then he turned and began to walk to the bucket. Slowly.

Sun removed himself to the far side of the paddock and paced slowly. Jo knew she should be thrilled at this progress. The horse and the man were actually communicating.

So why did she feel so terrible? No, not terrible. *Weird.* Her skin felt hot and her knees had yet to stop shaking and her heart was pounding fast.

Then Phillip was walking back toward her.

Oh, God. She wasn't sure she was strong enough for this. She'd spent the last ten years convincing herself that she could get through the nights without a drink or a man or a man holding a drink.

Phillip Beaumont was going to be her undoing.

"So," he said when he reached her again. He waved at the saddles. "What are we doing with the tack?"

"Cleaning it."

Instead of looking as if he had her right where he wanted her, he looked more off-balance. Good. She shouldn't be the only one off-balance here. "It's...not dirty."

"Do you want to ride?" His eyes widened in surprise and she realized what she'd said. "I mean, the horse. Do you want to ride the horse? *Sun.*"

Sweet merciful heavens, she could not be embarrassing herself more if she tried.

"Yes." But the way Phillip said it left the question of which kind of riding he was interested in doing wide open.

"Then you clean tack."

Seven

What did he want for a reward?

Phillip knew. He wanted to open his door tonight with a bottle of wine chilling on the table and then skip dinner entirely and head straight to the hot tub. He'd love to see how Jo's body filled out a bikini—or nothing at all. Nude was always fashionable.

He'd love his reward to go on for most of the evening. It'd been close to a week since he'd first woken up alone in his own bed and he missed having a woman to spend the evening with.

But that wasn't necessarily the reward he'd ask for.

He might ask for a kiss. That was a pretty big *might*. Her hand—warm and gentle but firm in his—had seemed to say that she was interested in a kiss. Combined with the entirely feminine blush that had pinked her cheeks? Yeah, a kiss would be good.

But he had to earn it first—by cleaning saddles, of all things. When was the last time he'd had to work so hard for something as simple as a kiss? He shouldn't be having fun. He should be frustrated that she was being so damned stubborn or insulted that his considerable charms were falling on mostly deaf ears.

But he wasn't. It struck him as beyond strange that he was actually enjoying the slow process of seducing Jo Spears.

So he cleaned a not-dirty saddle.

Normally, Phillip did not enjoy cleaning tack. It was his second least-favorite job on the farm, after shoveling stalls, the one he'd always had to do when he messed up.

But instead of feeling like a punishment, sitting on a blanket in the middle of a paddock taking apart a saddle and wiping it down—next to Jo—wasn't awful. In fact, it bordered on pleasant. The weather was beautifully sunny, with a bright breeze that ruffled the leaves on the trees.

As Phillip cleaned his saddle, he kept half an eye on the horse as he moved around the paddock. Sometimes he walked, sometimes he trotted, but he didn't race or buck or generally act like a horse that was out of control. That made Phillip feel pretty good.

But what made him feel better was the woman sitting next to him.

He had been patient and waited for her to touch him first. True, he hadn't been expecting her to grab his hand. He hadn't realized his hand had actually been moving. He'd been focused on not spooking Sun and trying to be still like she was. It'd taken a lot more energy than he'd anticipated. Who knew that standing still would be so hard?

Until she'd taken his hand. He realized she hadn't meant it as a come-on—but the way she'd reacted to his touch? The wall between them had busted wide open. She was attracted to him. He was interested in her.

Things were moving along nicely.

He kept cleaning the saddle until his feet started to fall

asleep. Boots were good for many things, but sitting on the ground wasn't one of them. "How long do we have to keep doing this?"

She leaned over to appraise his work. "Nice job."

"I had several years of practice."

"Really?" She stretched out her legs, which looked even longer and more muscular at this angle. What would it feel like to have legs that strong wrapped around his back? And how many saddles would he have to clean to find out? "How come?"

"Every time I did something wrong, I had to either clean tack or muck stalls. And when you're a hyper kid who's never had to follow rules before…" He shrugged. It was the truth, of course, but…he had never admitted that to another person.

He cleared his throat. "I cleaned a lot of tack. But it was good. I can harness the entire team of Percherons to the wagon myself."

She turned to look at him, an odd half-smile on her face. "What?"

"It's just that none of this," she replied, looking at the pile of polished leather they'd worked through, "fits with your public persona."

"There's more to me than just parties."

She grinned at him—a grin he was starting to recognize. She was about to give him some crap and she was going to enjoy doing it. He braced himself for the worst, but oddly, the fact that she was having fun made it not so bad.

"What would your lady friends say if they saw you sitting in the dirt?"

That's what she said. What he heard was superiority mixed in with a healthy dose of jealousy.

Jealous because she was interested.

Excellent. But he needed to move carefully here.

"I doubt they'd understand. Which is why they're not here." Only her. Before she could reload, he took control of the conversation. "Tell me about Betty."

Jo looked up, finding where her small donkey was now drinking from the bucket set at her height. "What do you want to know?"

"How long have you had her?" Yes, this was part of showing Jo there was more to him than a good time at a party or a family fortune. But he had to admit, he was curious.

"About ten years."

He supposed he shouldn't have been surprised by the short answer, but something in her tone indicated that perhaps not too many people had asked. "Where'd you get her?"

"My granny gave her to me." Jo sighed, as if the conversation were unavoidable and yet still painful. "I had…a rough patch. Granny thought I needed someone to keep me company. Most people would have gotten a puppy, but not Lina Throws Spears. She showed up with a donkey foal that only weighed twenty pounds." She grinned at the memory. "Itty Bitty Betty. We've been together ever since."

Phillip let that information sink in. There was a lot of it. How old was Jo? Given the faint lines around her eyes, he'd guess she wasn't in her twenties anymore.

What sort of rough patch had she had? Had someone broken her heart? That would certainly explain why she worked so hard at keeping that wall up between her and everyone else.

Letting Suzie go had hurt more than he'd expected— and that was before he'd read about her engagement to that prince. But to have a true broken heart, a man had to be in love.

After watching his parents and all of his stepparents and every horrid thing they did to each other in the name of love, Phillip would never do something as stupid as give his heart to anyone. Falling in love meant giving someone power to hurt you.

No love, no hurt. Just a long list of one-night stands that satisfied his needs quite well. Love was for the delusional. Lust was something honest and real and easily solved without risking hearts or family fortunes.

Also, what kind of name was Lina Throws Spears? Jo didn't look like an Indian—not like the ones in the movies, anyway. Her skin was tanned, but he'd always assumed that was because of the time she spent in the sun. She had a dusting of freckles across her nose and cheeks. Her hair was medium brown, not jet black.

Then there were her eyes. They were a pretty hazel color, light and soft in a woman who otherwise could appear hard.

On the other hand, there was that whole communing-with-the-animals thing she did. That certainly fit with his preconceived notions of American Indians.

"Yes?"

He quickly looked away. "What?"

Jo sighed again. "Go on. You know you're dying to ask."

"Throws Spears?"

"Granny—and my dad—are full-blooded Lakota Sioux. My mom's white. Any other questions?"

"You shortened your name?"

"My dad did."

Her tone brooked no warmth. Right. The topic of family was off-limits. He got that. His own family tree was so complicated that instead of a sturdy, upright oak it resembled a banyan tree that grew new trunks everywhere.

It was time to change the subject. "Where does Betty sleep?"

"If it's nice out, she stays in a pasture, but she's house trained," she said, nodding to the trailer.

"Really?"

That was a nice smile. "Really. I made a harness for her when we're driving. She sits up front. Likes to stick her nose out the window."

This bordered on the most ridiculous thing he had ever heard. "And you're sure she's a donkey and not a dog in disguise?"

"Very sure." She shot him a look that seemed to be the opposite of the hard tone she'd had when discussing her family. "Tomorrow, I'll saddle her up."

He looked at the small, fuzzy donkey. He couldn't quite imagine Betty with a saddle. "*Really?*" When Jo nodded, he added, "I…I look forward to seeing that."

She grinned. "Everyone does. Come on." Jo leaned back and stood, stretching her back. Which thrust out her chest.

From his angle, the view was amazing. His body responded with enthusiasm. Damn. This was going to make standing up even more difficult. "Where are we going?" It'd be nice if hot tubs or beds were the answer but somehow he knew it wouldn't be.

He managed to get to his feet, then leaned back down to grab his saddle. He'd spent close to an hour and a half getting the damned thing polished to a high shine.

"Leave it," Jo instructed.

"But I *cleaned* it."

"Leave it," she repeated in that no-nonsense tone. Then she began to walk to the gate.

"Better be a damn good reward," he muttered as he left all his hard work behind. He had a bad feeling about this.

Jo held the gate open for him, which meant it wasn't his fault that he had to pass close enough to her that he could count the freckles on her nose. She swung the gate behind him, but didn't step away. He didn't either. Close enough to touch, they both leaned against the now-closed gate. "Explain to me why we left the saddles in there? You know Sun is probably going to destroy them. Do you have any idea how much they cost?"

"You're already showing him you're not going to shoot him with a tranq gun or do anything else scary. Now you're going to show him that saddles and bridles are also not scary."

"But—"

"Shh." She had her eyes trained on the horse. "Just watch."

A damn good reward, he thought as he tried to rein in his irritation.

He watched. Trotting in looping circles, Sun looked at them, at the saddles and then at the bucket where Phillip had left the carrots.

Suddenly, Jo's fingers closed around his. "Be still," she said in that low voice again.

He hadn't realized he was moving, but did it matter? No, not with her fingers curling around his. Her touch did things to him—things that had nothing to do with being still and had everything to do with wanting to keep on moving—moving his lips over her fingers, her neck, her lips, his body moving over hers, with hers.

She must have felt it, too, because she turned her head toward him and favored him with one of those half-smiles.

He turned his hand over without letting go of her so they were palm-to-palm. He interlaced their fingers without looking away from Sun. After a moment, her hand relaxed into his.

It took everything he had to *not* lift her hand and press it to his lips, but he didn't. She'd made the first move and he'd countered with his own. Now it was her turn. If he skipped a turn, she might stop playing the game.

Then her fingers tightened on his. No mistaking it. They were holding hands in a way that had only the smallest of connections to what was happening in the paddock.

Not that the paddock wasn't interesting. Sun's loops were getting tighter and slower as he closed in on the bucket and carrots. Just when Phillip thought he would eat them, Sun spun and made straight for the saddles.

Oh, no. The horse hit the saddles with everything he had—and, considering he hadn't been bucking for hours on end, that was a lot. Phillip winced as Sun ground the saddles into the dirt.

The whole thing took less than five minutes. Betty stood off to the side, watching with an air of boredom. Then, head held high, Sun pranced over to the bucket and ate his carrots as if he'd planned it like that from the beginning.

"Some reward," Phillip muttered. He'd been upset about Sun before, but this was the first time he was out-and-out furious with the beast. That was an expensive saddle—and the one she'd been cleaning wasn't cheap, either. If his brother Chadwick knew that the horse trainer was letting Sun destroy several thousands of dollars of tack, he'd have her thrown off the premises. And possibly him, too.

"Stupid horse."

"Smart horse." Jo squeezed his hand, but that smile? That was for the horse.

"Why are you smiling? He ruined those saddles. *And* ate my carrots."

She notched an eyebrow as she cast him a sideways glance. The sudden burst of realization made him feel as if he'd been conned. "You *knew* he was going to do that?"

"Everyone's got to start somewhere," she replied, sounding lighthearted.

All that work for nothing. "Next time, he doesn't get carrots until he can behave himself." Even as he said the words, he knew they sounded ridiculous. Was he talking about a horse or a toddler? He glared at his multi-million dollar animal. "No rewards for that kind of attitude and that's final."

"Ah." Her voice—soft and, if he wasn't mistaken, nervous—snapped his attention back to where they were still palm-to-palm.

He had something coming to him, all the more so because she'd made him do all that work. He stroked his thumb along the length of her finger. He felt a light tremor, but she didn't pull away.

"Do I get my reward now? That saddle was very clean, right before it wasn't."

She tilted her head away, as if she were debating the merits of his argument. But he couldn't miss the way her lips were quirked into a barely contained smile.

"And I didn't even kill that horse when he trashed my tack," he reminded her as he leaned in.

She didn't lean away. "True." Her voice took on a sultry note, one that invited much more than holding hands. The pupils of her eyes widened; her gaze darted down to his lips. "Is this flirting?"

She was expecting him to kiss her, but something told him not to. Not yet. The longer he defied her expectations of him, the better the odds he'd wake up with her in his bed.

"It might be." He held her hand to his lips. A simple touch, skin against skin. Even though it about killed him not to take everything she was offering, he didn't.

Without breaking the contact between them, he raised his eyes to see Jo looking at him, her eyes wide with surprise and—he hoped—desire.

Raw need pumped through his blood. He almost threw his plans out the window and swept her into his arms. She was his, waiting for him to make his move....

She dropped her gaze. "What did you want for your reward?" The question could have been coy, but there was something else in her expression.

"All I wanted," he replied, not taking his eyes off her face, "was to see that beautiful blush on you."

Of course, that wasn't all he wanted. But it'd do for now. Then, to prove his point, he let her go and stepped back.

"That's…all?" The confusion that registered on her face was so worth it.

Clearly, not a lot of people had told her she was beautiful. What a crying shame. She had a striking look that was all her own. If that wasn't beautiful, he didn't know what was.

"Well…" He looked as innocent as he could. "I was supposed to clean a saddle. The saddle is, at this moment, quite dirty so I didn't really complete my task."

She blinked, managing to pull off coy in a cowboy hat. "Funny thing about that."

"What's funny?"

It shouldn't be right to find that little look of victory— one corner of her mouth quirked up into a smile, one eyebrow raised in challenge—so damned sexy, but he did. "Tomorrow morning—you, me and some saddles."

Phillip tried to stifle a groan, but he didn't manage it. "No."

"Yes." She paused, suddenly looking unsure of herself. "If you do a good job…"

He grinned on the inside but he kept his face calm. Oh, yeah—he had her right where he wanted her.

Almost, anyway.

Behind them, someone cleared his throat. Jo stiffened, a hard look wiping away anything sultry about her. She turned away and focused on Sun.

Phillip looked past her to see Richard standing a few feet away, hat in hands and an odd look on his face.

Damn. How long had he been standing there? Had he seen Phillip kiss her hand? It'd been easy to pretend that he and Jo were alone on the farm. The other hands steered well clear of her—probably because she'd told them to—and everyone more or less left him alone. The farm operated well enough without him.

But he and Jo weren't alone.

"I've got a farm to run," he said in a voice that was pitched just loud enough for Richard to hear. "I'll stop by later to see how you're getting on with Sun."

She nodded, looking as uninterested as physically possible.

She could hide the truth from Richard, but not from him.

Eight

Jo sat at the dinette table in her trailer that night, not seeing her email. She was supposed to be replying to horse owners who were looking for a miracle, but that's not what she was doing.

Phillip Beaumont had kissed her hand. And nothing more.

If that were her only problem, it would have been enough. But it wasn't. She wasn't sure how much Richard had seen.

For the first time in a very long time, Jo was…unsure of herself. One man who, by all accounts, was a spoiled party boy with more money than sense and she had apparently lost her damned mind.

She did not fool around with clients. Under any circumstances. Beyond being a temptation back into her old ways, it was bad for business. If word got around that she was open to affairs, people might stop hiring her.

What a mess. If flirting with Phillip Beaumont was

causing such a problem for her, why on God's green Earth was she letting it go on?

Because she'd seen the look on his face when she'd hinted that if he cleaned another saddle tomorrow morning, he'd get another reward.

She should have jerked her hand out of his when he kissed it. Hell, she shouldn't have touched him at all. She should have followed her own rules—rules she had in place for a variety of exceptionally good reasons—and steered well clear of Phillip Beaumont and his reputation.

If she didn't feel such a duty to Sun, she'd pack up and drive off to another, less tempting job tomorrow. Yes, it'd be a blow to her reputation to lose Beaumont Farms as a reference, but three other trainers had already failed. Bailing on this job wouldn't end her aspirations, not like having an affair with Phillip could.

But she wouldn't abandon the horse, not when they were making such progress. Richard had told her that if she couldn't save the horse, he'd have to be put down. True, Sun might have calmed to the point where another trainer could come in and finish the job, but she didn't know if she wanted to hope for the best and never look back. That's what the old her would have done. That's not what the woman she was now did.

Her only consolation was that she had rediscovered her restraint this afternoon when Phillip had driven past the paddock with a wagon full of hay to ask if she wanted to see his Thoroughbreds. Then he'd held the reins out to her.

She'd passed on his offer, saying she needed to keep an eye on Sun.

This would be so much easier if Phillip were a jerk. Some of the men—and women—who'd hired her were, in fact, total jerks. That's why she had that upfront policy of not hooking up or dating. That's why she kept her trailer door locked.

But Phillip wasn't a jerk. At least, not once he'd sobered up.

He cleaned tack because she asked him to. He tried to be still because it was important to Sun, even if he didn't totally succeed. He let her drive his Percheron team. Hell, he brought her coffee.

That wasn't jerkiness. That was thoughtfulness.

She had no idea how to respond to it.

Crap, she was in so much trouble.

This was a sign of how far she'd come. The old Jo would have embraced the trouble she was in and gone looking for more. She shouldn't beat herself up for encouraging Phillip, not really. She should be proud of the fact that she'd resisted his considerable charms and good looks thus far.

Now she just had to keep doing that.

In the midst of losing to herself in a debate, she heard something that sounded suspiciously like shouting. Loud, but muffled, shouting.

She scowled at the clock. That wasn't right. It was close to ten in the evening. The hired hands had all gone home before five. The whole farm was usually quiet at night, with the exception of the guards who checked the barns every other hour.

Not this evening. The shouting was louder now. She could make out two different voices.

Betty, she thought in a panic. The weather was supposed to be clear, so Jo had left the little donkey out in the pasture across the drive from Sun's paddock.

Moving fast, she slipped her jeans back on and shoved her feet into her boots. Thankfully, she hadn't taken her shirt off yet, so she didn't have to mess with the buttons. She left the trailer and grabbed her pistol from the glove box, tucking it into the back of her waistband. If someone was trying to take Betty or Sun or any other horse on this property, she wanted to catch them in the act. Then she could hold them until the guards came back around. She'd interrupted attempted robberies before. She knew how to handle her weapon.

She slipped along the side of her trailer and peeked out. A pair of headlights pointed into Sun's paddock and the horse was going nuts.

Two men were arguing in front of the headlights. She realized with a start that one of the men was Phillip. The other was slightly taller, slightly broader and had a slightly deeper voice but otherwise, he could have been Phillip's twin.

Chadwick Beaumont? Who else could it be?

Keeping to the shadows, she edged closer. They weren't trying to be quiet but she was having trouble making out what they were arguing about.

"...be insane!" Phillip yelled as he paced away then spun back to face his brother.

"The company—and, I might add, the family—cannot afford to keep standing idle while you throw good money after bad and you know it." Chadwick's voice was level, bordering on cruel. This was not a man who could be easily moved.

Phillip was anything but level. "The Percherons are not throwing money away," he shouted, flinging his hands around as if he were throwing money around. "They're our brand name!"

"Are they?" Chadwick sneered. "I thought *you* were our brand name. The face of Beaumont Beer. God knows you stick that face out enough."

Behind them, Sun made a noise that was closer to a scream than a whinny. Jo winced. How long would it take for the horse to calm down after this?

But the men didn't notice the horse. They were too lost in their argument.

Phillip threw up his hands. "Do you know what it'll do

to our public goodwill if we get rid of the Percherons? Do you have *any* idea?"

"This farm costs millions of dollars to operate," Chadwick countered so smoothly that Jo didn't have any doubt he'd anticipated this defense. "And all your pet projects cost several million more." At this, he threw a glance toward Sun, who was flat-out racing, just like he'd been the day Jo had shown up. The way Chadwick looked at the horse made Jo think that, if he'd been in charge, he would have let Richard put the animal down without hesitation. "To say nothing of all your little 'escapades.'"

As he paced, Phillip groaned. It was the sort of noise a man might make if he'd been punched in the kidneys. "Do you understand nothing about marketing? For God's sake, Chadwick—even Matthew—could explain how this works! People love the Percherons. *Love* them. And you want to just throw that all away?"

"Love," Chadwick intoned, "doesn't run a company."

Phillip whipped back to his brother, his fists balled. Jo flinched. If they started to brawl, she'd have to break them up. "You got that right, you heartless bastard. Can your bean-counting brain wrap itself around the damage you'll cost us with consumers? The Percherons are a part of this company, Chadwick. You can't sell them off any more than you can sell the company."

The silence that fell between the two men was so cold that Jo shivered.

"I already sold the company."

Jo's mouth dropped open, just as Phillip's had. "You… *what?*" Jo wasn't sure she'd ever heard Phillip sound so wounded. She couldn't blame him.

"I'm not going to work myself into an early grave so that I can pay for your failed horses or Frances's failed art or even Byron's failed romances," Chadwick said in a voice as hard as iron. "I've worked for ten years to keep the Beaumont family going and I'm sick of it. AllBev made an offer. The board accepted it. It's *done*. We'll announce when the lawyers give us the go-ahead."

Phillip gaped at him. "But…you…Dad…the company!"

"Hardwick Beaumont is dead, Phillip. He's been dead for years. I don't have to prove myself to him anymore and neither do you." Something in Chadwick's tone changed. For a moment, he sounded…kind. It was at such odds with the hard man she'd been listening to that Jo had to shake her head to make sure the same person was speaking. "I'm getting married."

"You're *what?* Aren't you already married?"

"My ex-wife is now just that—my ex. I'm starting over, Phillip. I'm going to be happy. You should do the same. Figure out who you are if you aren't Hardwick's second son."

Phillip's mouth open, closed, then opened again. "You can't sell the farm. You can't, Chadwick. Please. I need this place. I need the horses. Without them…"

Chadwick was unmoved. Anything that might have been understanding or brotherly was gone. "The new owners of the Brewery have no desire to take on the sinking money pit that is this farm. They do not want the Percherons and I can't afford them. I can't afford *you*."

Jo must have gasped or stepped on a twig or something because suddenly both men spun.

"Who's there?" they demanded in unison.

She stepped into the edge of the light. "It's me. Jo."

Phillip gave her something that might have been a smile. Chadwick only glared. "Who?" He turned his attention to Phillip. "Who's she?"

Phillip's shoulders slumped in defeat. "Jo Spears. The horse trainer who's saving Sun."

Jo nodded her head in appreciation. He'd gotten the saving part right.

Chadwick was not impressed. "Now you're keeping women on the farm?" He made a noise of disgust. "And how much is this costing?"

Jo bristled. Clearly, Chadwick Beaumont did not have his brother's way with words *or* women.

When Phillip didn't answer, Chadwick shook his head in disgust. He said, "I only came out here to warn you because we're family. If I were you, I'd start getting rid of the *excess*—" he looked at Sun, then at Jo "—as soon as possible on your own terms. Save yourself the embarrassment of a public auction." He walked back to his car. "If you don't, I will."

Then Chadwick Beaumont slammed the door shut, put the shiny little sports car in reverse, and peeled out.

Phillip dropped his head.

And stood absolutely still.

Chadwick was going to sell the horses. All of them. Not just Sun or the Appaloosas or even the Thoroughbreds, but *all* of them. The Beaumont Percherons—a self-sustaining herd of about a hundred horses that went back a hundred and twenty-three years—would be gone. The farm would be gone. The farmhouse that his great-grandfather had built as a refuge from the rest of the world— gone. And what would Phillip have once the horses and the farm were gone?

Nothing. Not a damned thing.

God, he needed a drink.

Sun made that unholy noise again, but Phillip couldn't even look. It was so tempting to blame Sun for this. The horse had cost seven million dollars. He'd never seen his brother so mad as when Phillip had told Chadwick about the horse. If only Sun hadn't cost so much....

But that was a cop-out and he knew it. Phillip was the one who'd bought the horse. And all the other horses. And the tack, the wagons, the carriages. He was the one who'd hired the farm hands. And Jo.

Jo.

Almost as if he'd called her, she came to stand next to him. Her hand slipped into his and her fingers intertwined with his. She felt…smaller than she had this afternoon.

He felt smaller.

"Come on," she said in that low voice that brooked no arguments. She gave his hand a gentle tug and he stumbled after her.

She led him to her trailer. Any other time, Phillip would have been excited about this development. But he couldn't even think about sex right now. Not when he was on the verge of losing everything he'd worked for.

She basically pulled him up the narrow trailer steps and then pushed him toward a small dinette table. "Have a seat."

He sat. Heavily. *Jesus.* He knew that the company was in trouble. But he had no idea that Chadwick would do this. That he'd even been considering selling the Brewery, much less the farm. He'd thought…Chadwick would win. That's what Chadwick did. He'd fight off the acquisition and save the company and everything would continue on as it had before.

But Chadwick hadn't. Wouldn't. He was going to get rid of the farm. Of Phillip.

This was…this was his home. Not the Beaumont family mansion, not the apartment in the city. The farm was where he'd always felt the most normal. *Been* the most normal. He'd been able to do something that had made him proud. Had made his father proud of him. Hardwick Beaumont had never had a second look for his second son out in the real world. But here, talking horses, his father had noticed him. Told him he'd done a good job. Been so proud of him.

And now it was going to be taken away from him.

Jo made some noise. Phillip looked up to see her filling an electric kettle, a small handgun set on the counter next to her. "What?"

"Making tea," she said in that same low and calming and ridiculously self-assured voice—the one she used when she was working with Sun.

He laughed, even though there was nothing funny about tea. "Got any whiskey to go with that? I could use a drink."

She paused while reaching into a cabinet. The pause lasted only a moment, but he felt the disapproval anyway.

He didn't care. He needed a drink. Several drinks. Maybe a fifth of drinks. He couldn't deal with losing the farm. With his horses. With Sun. Everything.

"I don't have any whiskey."

"I'll settle for vodka."

"I don't have anything but tea and a couple of cans of soda."

He laughed again. The universe seemed hell-bent on torturing him.

The kettle whistled—a noise that seemed to drive straight into his temple. Everything was too much right now—too much noise, too much light. Too much Jo sliding into the seat opposite him, looking at him with those big, pretty eyes of hers. His hands started to shake.

"Here." She slid a steaming mug toward him.

He looked at the tea. Insult to injury, that's what this was. It wasn't enough that he was about to lose everything he held dear. He had to have a horse trainer rub his nose in it.

The anger that peaked above the despair felt good. Well, not good—but better than the horrible darkness that was trying to swallow him inside out. "I've got whiskey at the house, you know. You're not stopping me from drinking."

She held her mug in her hands and blew on the tea, her

gaze never leaving his face. "No," she agreed, sounding too damned even, "I'm not."

"And I'm not some damned horse, either, so stop doing that whole calm-and-still bullshit," he snapped.

If she was offended, she didn't show it. Instead, she sipped the tea. "Does that help?"

"Jesus, you're doing it again. Does *what* help?"

"The blackout. Does that help?"

"It's a hell of a lot better than *this*." Logically, he knew he wasn't mad at her. She hadn't done anything but the job he'd hired her for.

But his world was ending and Chadwick was gone. Someone had to pay. And Jo was here.

"Don't you ever get tired of it?"

"You think you know me?" he said. Except it came out louder than he meant it to. "You don't know anything about me, so you can stop acting superior. You have no idea what my life is like."

"Any more than you have an idea of mine?"

He glared at her. "Fine. Just get it off your chest. Go ahead and tell me that I'm throwing my life away one drink at a time and alcohol never solved anything and blah, blah, blah."

She shrugged.

"I can stop whenever I want," he snapped.

"You just don't want to."

"I *want* a damn drink." Water pricked at his eyes. "You wouldn't understand."

"Yes," she said and this time he heard something different in her voice. "I would."

He looked up at her. She met his gaze without blinking and without deflecting. Her nose, he noticed again. It'd been broken. Without the shadows cast by her hat, it was easier to see the bump on the bridge that didn't match the rest of her.

She was beautiful. If she wasn't going to get him some whiskey, she could still sleep with him. Sex was always fine with him. He'd been chasing her for a week now with nothing more than a kiss on the hand to show for it. He could lose himself in this woman and it might make him feel better. At least for a little while.

She turned her head in one direction, then the other, giving him a better look at her nose. "I stopped."

The compliment he'd loaded up came to a screeching halt. "Stopped what?"

She set her mug down and slid out of her seat. "There was never a good reason. My parents are normal, happily married. No abuse, no alcoholism. I wasn't shy or awkward or even that rebellious." She stood and undid the top button on her shirt.

As her fingers undid the second button, his pulse began to pound. What the hell? He hadn't even busted out the compliment and she was undressing? All his hard work was paying off. He was about to get lucky. Thank God. Then he wouldn't have to think.

Except...this wasn't right. First off, there was far too much talking. But beyond that, Jo—just stripping? Jesus, he must be so messed up right now, because this wasn't how he wanted her. He didn't want her to give it up just to make him feel better. He wanted her to want him as much as he wanted her.

He didn't get the chance to tell her to wait. She went on, "Dad's Lakota, so I had my fair share of people who called me a half-breed, but doesn't everyone get teased for something?" Another button popped open.

Why was she telling him this? Even if she was trying to seduce him, this didn't seem like the proper way to go about it. But he could just see the swell of her breasts peek over the top of the shirt.

She undid another button. Unlike her nose, her breasts

were perfect. He opened his mouth to tell her just that, to try and get this seduction back on track, but he didn't get any further.

"I had my first drink in seventh grade at a Fourth of July party. A wine cooler I snagged. I opened it up and poured it into a cup and told everyone it was pink lemonade. It was good. I liked it. So I had another. And another."

She undid the last button and stood there. The curves of her breasts were tantalizingly at eye level, but she didn't move toward him, didn't shimmy or shake or anything a normal woman might have done. He leaned forward. If he could touch her, fill his hands with her soft skin and softer body, they could get to the part where they were both naked and he wasn't thinking about anything but sex. About her. That's what he wanted, wasn't it?

She turned her back to him. "By the time I was in high school, I was the resident party girl. I don't know how I graduated and I don't know how I didn't get pregnant. I have no idea how I got into college, but I did. I don't know if I ever went to a class sober. I don't remember going to that many classes."

The shirt began to slide down.

Phillip began to sweat. He tried to focus on what she was saying and not the body she was unwrapping for him, but it was a damned hard thing to attempt—a fact that was directly connected with other damned hard things happening to him right now.

"I'd wake up and not know where I was, who I was with. College guys, older guys—men I didn't know. I couldn't remember meeting them or going home with them." She shrugged, a bare shoulder going up and down. The movement pushed the shirt down even farther. "Couldn't remember the sex—couldn't remember if I wanted it or not."

Phillip tensed, torn between despair, desire and sheer confusion. Confusion won. Instead of a swath of smooth skin, Jo was revealing a back covered in puckers and ripples.

"I'd stumble back to my room and scan my phone for pictures or messages. For the memories, I told myself, but there were things I'd done…" She paused, but it was only the barest hint of emotion. "Facing them—no. It was easier to find another party and tell myself I was having a good time than it was to accept what I'd done. What I'd become."

The shirt fell off her right arm, revealing the true extent of the damage. Most of her back was scarred—horrible marks that went below the waistband of her pants. She tilted her head to the left and lifted her shoulder-length hair. Even her hairline was messed up—rough and uneven where the scars stole farther up. "The only reason I know his name is because my granny saved the article. Tony Holmes. He ran a red light, got T-boned so hard by a big SUV that it flipped the car. He wasn't buckled in. I was."

She tilted her body so he could see the contours of her back. Hidden among the mass of twisted skin were other scars—long, neat ones that looked surgical. "The car caught fire, but they got me out in time."

"Tony?"

For the first time in this dry recitation of facts, she seemed to feel something. "He wouldn't have felt the flames anyway."

Jesus. His stomach turned. This wasn't some crazy, "let's get in touch with our feelings" kind of talk. This was serious—life and death.

He didn't want to believe her—he'd never wanted to believe anything less in his life—but there was no arguing with the scars.

It could have been me, he thought. The realization made him dizzy. It *could* have been him—the wild party he didn't remember, the strange person buckled in next to him that he wouldn't have remembered, either. There was only

one reason something like that hadn't happened. He wished
to God that reason was because he was a responsible man.

But it wasn't. No, Ortiz—his driver—was the reason.
His brothers Chadwick and Matthew had decreed that Phillip would have a driver whenever he was at a company-sponsored event. It was company policy.

A company policy that no one else in the company had
to follow.

"My back was broken in two places. I shouldn't be able
to walk. I shouldn't even be alive." She turned to the side
to grab the shirt from where it hung off her left arm. Phillip caught a glimpse of her breast, full and heavy and his
dick responded to the sight of her bare breast before she got
ahold of her shirt and snapped the buttons back together.

But all he felt was cold and shaky. His head was pounding as if he had a hangover. He still wanted a drink. He
dug the heels of his hands into his eyes, trying to block
out the images she'd put there on purpose—images of her
waking up with strangers, never really knowing what had
happened. Of her trapped in a burning car next to a dead
man. "I'm not like that."

"Because you don't drive?"

He nodded. He'd never been with anyone who'd died
after a good party. He never did anything with anyone
who didn't want it.

He felt the dinette shift as she sat back down at the table.
It'd be safe to look at her. But he couldn't. He couldn't
move.

"Between the back surgeries and the burn care, I was in
traction in the hospital for months," she went on, as if he
needed more torture. "It was a year before I could move
without pain. And because I *am* an alcoholic, I never even
got the good painkillers. I had to feel it all. Everything I'd
done. Everything I was. I couldn't hide from it."

"How do you stand it?" Why did he have to sound as

though she was twisting the knife in his gut a quarter-turn at a time?

Because that's what she was doing. Twisting.

Except she wasn't, not really. More like she was holding up a mirror so he could see the knife he was twisting himself.

"I stopped. Stopped drinking, stopped sleeping around, stopped fighting it."

"What if…" He swallowed. *What if he couldn't stop?*

He heard the seat rustle as she leaned back. "Did you spike your coffee this morning?"

"No." But he was really wishing he had. Anything to numb the pain.

"What about yesterday?"

He shook his head. He'd thought he felt hopeless after Chadwick had driven off. But now?

He didn't know if he was coming or going.

"It's now…10:53. Another hour and seven minutes and you'll have made it through two days." She had the nerve to sound optimistic about this fact. "That's as good a place to start as any."

"Is this the part where I'm supposed to say 'One day at a time' and we sing 'Kumbaya' and then we talk about steps?"

"Nope."

"Good. Because I don't want to hear it."

"Our kind never does."

"We are not the same kind, Jo." But even as he said it, he knew it was a lie. The only difference was that she'd stopped and he hadn't.

"No," she agreed. "I have the scars to prove it."

"Does it…does it still hurt?" He didn't know if he was asking about the scars on her back or the other kind of scars.

"Not really. I have Betty now. She helps. It's only when…"

Something in her voice—something longing and wistful—made him pull his hands away from his face.

Jo was looking at him. That wasn't a surprise. The trailer was small and they were talking. But it was *how* she was looking at him. Gone was the unnatural calm.

Sitting across from him was a woman who wanted something that she would never allow herself to have.

Him.

She looked away first. "He wants you to give up," she told him as she studied the bottom of her mug.

Phillip was still trying to figure out that look, so her words took him completely off guard. "What?"

"Your brother. He expects you to run off and get so drunk that he can do whatever he wants with *your* farm and *your* animals and you won't be able to put up a fight." When she looked back up again, whatever longing he'd seen in her eyes was gone.

"What should I do?"

"That's not my place." She gave him a tight smile. "You have to decide for yourself. Fight or give up, it doesn't matter to me."

"It doesn't?" It hurt to hear that, but he wasn't sure why. "Not even a little?"

She gave him a long look. He got the feeling she wanted to say something else, but she didn't.

Finally, she said, "Can you live with yourself if you let the farm go without a fight?"

Phillip dropped his head into his hands again. This was the only place he'd ever been happy—where he was still happy, even though his father was dead and gone.

He didn't know who he was without the farm to come back to. The Phillip Beaumont that put on suits and went to parties—he didn't remember half of what that Phillip did.

He'd been telling himself that not remembering was the sign of a good time for how long? Years.

Decades.

Even if he fought for the farm, as she said, he wasn't sure he could live with himself.

"I need this place."

"Then fight for it."

He nodded, letting the words roll around in his head. They bounced off memories of Dad lifting him onto the back of a Percheron named Sally and leading him down the drive. Of piping up as Dad and his trainer argued over a Thoroughbred to say that Daddy should buy the horse because he ran fast—and having Dad pat him on the head with a smile as he said, "My Phillip's got a good head for horses."

Memories of buying his first Thoroughbred and watching it win its first race in the owner's box with Dad.

Of buying the Appaloosas over Dad's objections, then overhearing Dad tell the farm manager that the horses were better than he expected, but he should have known because Phillip always did have a good head for horses.

Of harnessing up the Percheron team himself for Dad's funeral and driving the team of ten in the procession over the objections of every single member of his family because that was how he chose to honor his father.

When he wasn't on the farm…he had nothing. Vague snippets of dancing and drinking and having sex with nameless, faceless women. Headaches and blackouts and checking his phone in a panic the next morning to see what he'd done.

"If I go back to the house, I'll get the whiskey."

Just saying it out loud was an admission of failure. It was also the truth. He didn't know which was worse.

He heard Jo take a deep breath. "If I make up a bed for

you, you understand that's not an invitation?" She exhaled. "It's not that I'm not…" her voice trailed off.

Interested.

She was interested. Here, in the safety of her trailer, with all their cards on the table, she wasn't going to hide it. "It has to be this way," she went on, sounding as hopeless as he'd ever heard her. "I gave up men when I gave up drinking."

He nodded even though he couldn't remember spending the night with a woman that didn't involve sex. "You'd let me stay? Why?"

The smile she gave him was sadder than anything he'd ever seen on her face. "Because," she said, leaning forward and placing her hand on top of his. "No one's past saving. Not even you."

But as quick as she'd touched him, she pulled away and was standing up. "I'll be right back."

He blinked up at her. "Where are you going?"

Jo stood. He didn't miss that she grabbed the gun off the counter and shoved it into her waistband. "I need to check on Sun and get Betty. She's good for nights like this."

He managed a small smile. "I'll be here."

No one was past saving. Not even him.

He didn't know if he should laugh or cry at that.

Jo stopped halfway down the steps and shot him that side-eye look. "Good," was all she said.

Then she was out the door.

Nine

Jo did not sleep.

She lay in her bed, listening to the sounds of Phillip also not sleeping. She could tell he wasn't sleeping by the way the trailer creaked with every toss and turn and also by the way that Betty would occasionally shake her head and exhale heavily.

Even without Betty's added exasperation, Jo would have been aware of every single one of Phillip's movements. She hadn't been this close to a man in, well…since before the accident.

She felt as if she'd walked into a bar and bellied up to the counter, only to nurse a Sprite. How was she supposed to make it through the night without falling back into her old ways?

Around two in the morning, Phillip shifted again. That noise was followed by the distinctive sound of the floors squeaking as he walked. Jo tensed. It wasn't a huge trailer. Where was he going?

Not here. Not to her. If he opened the sliding door and told her he couldn't get through the night and he needed her, she didn't think she'd be strong enough to direct him back to the dinette table that had converted into a too-small bed.

The footsteps stopped in the middle of the trailer, then she heard the fridge open up. Then the fridge door shut and his steps went back to the front of the trailer. She heard the cushions sag as he sat, then heard Betty shake her head.

She could see him sitting there, rubbing Betty's ears as he struggled. How many nights had she done the same thing?

She remembered when she'd finally been cleared to drive by herself. She'd made up some excuse to run to the grocery store, only to have her dad say, "Don't forget, Joey." Her mom had met her at the front door, car keys in hand. But instead of stopping her or announcing she was coming along, Mom had just wrapped Jo in a hug and said, "Don't forget, sweetie."

They hadn't stopped her. If they had, who knows—she might have tried harder to go around them. But they didn't. They made it clear it was her choice and hers alone.

So she'd stood there in the booze aisle at the convenience store and stared at the bottles of amber liquid. It would have been so easy to buy one can, slam it in the car and throw the can away. No one would have known.

Except…she would have known.

Jo had gone home empty-handed to find her granny, Lina, sitting on the front porch with a twenty-pound donkey on her lap. Lina had pulled Jo into a strong hug, taken a deep breath—to check for the smell of booze, no doubt—and asked, "Did you remember what you were looking for?"

"Yeah." She'd expected a greater sense of accomplishment. She'd stopped. She'd walked away. She was a stronger, better person now.

But all she'd felt was drained. How was she going to make the same choice every day for the rest of her life? She didn't think she could do it.

"This here is Itty Bitty Betty," Lina had said, plopping the donkey into Jo's lap. "She needs someone to look after her."

Jo sighed, doing some tossing and turning of her own. Betty was mellower now, less prone to taking corners too fast and crashing into walls. But she still had the same soft ears, the same understanding eyes. She kept Jo grounded.

Except that Betty was out there with Phillip—and Phillip was still not sleeping. Jo couldn't sleep if he didn't sleep.

She could open up the sliding screen that separated her bedroom from the rest of the camper and sit with him. She could wrap her hand around his and then he'd be still.

But she didn't. She didn't fix people and she couldn't save them and she sure as hell wasn't going to put herself in a position where she might kiss him because if she kissed him, she wasn't sure she could stop at just one kiss. She'd never been able to stop at just one.

And if she didn't stop at one kiss, what was to say she'd be able to stop at a couple of kisses? Or that she'd not run her hands over his body? That she wouldn't lean into his groan and tilt her head back, encouraging him to kiss her on that spot where her neck met her shoulders?

She kept the door firmly shut. And did not sleep.

At six, she heard him get up again. Groggy from lack of sleep, she wondered if she should make coffee for him. But before she could get her feet on the floor, the door opened and shut and the trailer was still.

Phillip was gone.

Somehow, she knew she'd be cleaning tack alone today.

* * *

Phillip was waiting at the door when Matthew drove up.

"Took you long enough."

Matthew gave him a tired smile. "Something came up at work. I need a drink."

"Uh..."

Matthew turned. "Problem?"

"I don't have any alcohol in the house."

Matthew studied him, taking in everything from the boots to the jeans before finally staring him in the eye. "Either you drank everything you already had or..."

It wasn't the observation that hurt so much as the fact that it could have been true. "I had Richard come get all my booze and give it to the hands."

"You did?"

Phillip nodded. "I, uh, I'm trying to drink less. Or not at all."

"Is that so." It wasn't a question.

"Yeah...." Although a drink would be nice right now. When had it gotten so hard to talk to his brother? "A friend helped me realize if I wanted to keep the farm, I had to be sober to do it."

Matthew rubbed his eyes. "And when did this start?"

"Yesterday." Phillip swallowed.

"Good start." He almost sounded sincere. "I can't wait to meet this 'friend' of yours."

"She's down at the barn. With Sun."

Matthew rubbed his temples. "The seven-million dollar horse?"

"Yes."

There was a long pause. Phillip's stomach caved in. This was too much—he couldn't deal. What the hell had he been thinking? He couldn't even handle Matthew. He had to have been out of his mind to think he could confront Chadwick.

"She?"

Phillip nodded.

"You're going to screw up Chadwick's deal because you're trying to get *laid*?"

"I'm trying to save my farm," Phillip shot back. "Besides, correct me if I'm wrong, but aren't you about to lose your job if his deal goes through? I can't imagine that new owners would want a Beaumont vice president of whatever it is you do."

"Public relations," Matthew snapped, glaring at Phillip. "Which means I get to manage you whenever you go off the rails. Lucky freaking *me*."

"I didn't go off the rails," Phillip promised. "Chadwick showed up here and said he was going to sell all my horses, the whole farm—what was I supposed to do? Go drink myself into oblivion? This is my life, Matthew. This is…" His voice caught. "This is the only part of me that's *real*. And you know it. I can't let it go."

"You're serious, aren't you?"

"Of course I'm serious. I need your help. Chadwick won't listen to me. I doubt he'll even listen to a poll with the tens of thousands of votes to keep the Percherons. You're the only one of us he trusts."

That was the right thing to say. Sure, Matthew raised an eyebrow as if he was certain Phillip were feeding him a line of bull, but the pissed-off look softened. "You really don't have anything to drink in the house?"

"I had my cleaning service go through my apartment, too."

Matthew nodded. "Okay. Tell me your plan. You do have one, right?"

Phillip took a deep breath. "I want to buy the farm from the company."

The hours he'd had to wait for Matthew had been filled

with frantic planning. Because if the farm stayed with the company, he'd still lose it. That was unacceptable.

But if he bought the farm, well, he could *lease* the Percherons back to the Brewery. The company would have all the marketing benefits of the Percheron team without having to carry the expense of the farm on the balance sheet.

It could work. Except for two little details. Matthew was staring at him, mouth open. Finally, he got himself under control. "Do you know how much that will cost? The land alone is probably worth five, ten million dollars."

"Eight. Eight million for three hundred acres, seven barns, twelve outbuildings and one house."

Matthew eyed him suspiciously. "And the horses?"

"About fifteen to twenty thousand a piece, just for the Percherons. I've got a hundred, so that's another one to two million. The total value of all the horses on the farm, including Kandar's Golden Sun and the Thoroughbreds, is between fifteen and twenty million. The hitches, tractors and other things are maybe another million, plus the ongoing cost of hired help, grain, and other overhead."

Phillip cleared his throat. So it wasn't such a little detail. "To buy the whole thing outright would be thirty million. To buy it piecemeal at auction might push it as high as fifty million. People would want a part of the Beaumont name."

For once in his life, Matthew did not have a snarky comeback to that. He shook his head before finally speaking. "You've done your homework. That worries me."

A sense of pride warmed the cockles of Phillip's heart. He'd managed to impress his younger brother. "The farm is mostly self-sustaining," he went on. "I sell a lot of horses. If I leased the Percherons back to the company, maybe started charging a nominal fee for parade appearances, that'd cover a lot of the cost. And Sun…well, the stud fees alone are going to earn back his purchase price."

That was all true. With some judicious management

and perhaps selling off some additional horses, the farm could break even.

Which still left one little problem.

"Do you have thirty million?" Matthew asked.

"Not exactly. I hoped Chadwick might cut me a deal, seeing as we're family."

Matthew gave him a look that didn't put much stock in brotherly love. "How much do you have?"

That little sticking point was stuck all right—in Phillip's throat. "I'd sell the apartment in the city and live here full time. Downsize my wardrobe, cars—everything. That'd bring in a million, maybe two."

"How much," Matthew said, carefully enunciating each word, "do you have?"

"Plus, I'd get my share of the company sale, right? I have executive benefits. How much is that worth?"

Matthew gave him a look better suited to their father. "You *might* get fifteen million. That's sixteen, seventeen million tops. I don't know if 'brotherly love' would cover the other twelve."

Phillip forced himself to breathe as Matthew scowled. "It's the best I can do."

"That's it?" Matthew said it in the kind of dismissive tone that made it sound as if they were talking about hundreds, not millions. "That's all you've got? You don't have any other assets? Stocks?"

Phillip shook his head.

"Property?" When Phillip shook his head again, Matthew groaned. "Nothing?"

"I drank it all."

His brother rubbed his temples again, as if that would provide the solution. "You realize Chadwick's still bitter about the seven-million-dollar horse?"

"Yeah, I realize."

"He's going to make you pay him back for that horse. You're aware of that."

"Yeah." This is what defeat tasted like. Bitter.

But, really, did he deserve any less? He'd spent most of a lifetime being a pain in Chadwick's ass.

When it came to horses, Phillip could finally beat his older brother. For a few hours a month, he was Hardwick's golden son. He'd done everything in his power to make sure that Chadwick never forgot it.

Even bought a horse named Kandar's Golden Sun. Just because he could. Because that's what Hardwick would have done.

But their father was dead and gone. Had been for years. Why had it only been in the last six days that Phillip had tried to figure out who he was if he wasn't Hardwick Beaumont's second son?

It'd been because of Jo, because she hadn't seen Hardwick's forgotten second child. She'd seen a man who had a good head for horses—a man who could be weak and stupid, yes, a man who drank too much and remembered too little. She hadn't seen a man she could fix.

She'd seen a man worth saving.

"Matthew," Phillip said, suddenly unsure of what he was going to say. "I'm sorry."

Matthew glared at him. "You should be. This is one hell of a mess."

"No," Phillip went on, trying to find some steel for his resolve. "I'm *not* sorry about trying to save the farm. I'll do anything to save this place. I'm…I'm sorry about everything else. I'm sorry your job is managing me when I go off the rails. I'm sorry I go off the rails sometimes—" Matthew shot him a mean look. "All the time. I'm sorry I don't remember half the stuff I've done because I blacked out."

"Phillip," Matthew said, sounding uncharacteristically nervous.

"No, let me finish." Finishing was suddenly important. Phillip had been so mad at Chadwick, he'd never taken the time to understand why the man was so mad at him. But he could see it now, cleared of the haze of drinking. "I'm sorry you were always in between me and Chadwick. *Are* always in between us. I'm—I'm sorry I hated you when you were a kid."

Matthew stared at him. "What?"

"I'm a terrible brother. I blamed you for my mother going away but you were just a kid. It wasn't your fault and it wasn't fair of me to blame you."

They stood there, staring at each other as Phillip's words settled around them. He felt as if he should say something else but he didn't know what. Of course, he hadn't known he was going to say that, either.

"Why are you saying all of this?"

Phillip shrugged. Truthfully, he didn't know. Only... he needed to. He couldn't live with himself if he didn't.

"I don't want to be the kind of guy who has to have someone else clean up his messes anymore. I want to manage myself, my own life from here on out." He swallowed again. "I'm sorry it took me this long to figure that out."

"You..." Matthew cleared his throat and straightened his shoulders. "You were just a kid, too. It wasn't your fault."

Phillip shook his head. "Maybe when we were six, but we're not anymore. We're grown men and I've been—well, I've been an asshole and I'm sorry."

Matthew walked away from him. He didn't go far, maybe five paces before he stopped and dropped his head, but in that moment, Phillip felt hopelessness clawing at him. It'd seemed like a good idea. A *necessary* one. But....

"You can't hide out here forever. You're still contractually obligated to represent Beaumont Breweries at events. If you have any hope of convincing Chadwick to go along with your plan, you've got to hold up your end of the bargain. You're still the—what was it? The 'handsome face of the Beaumont Brewery'."

"I know." That was the other little detail that wasn't little. He knew that if he stayed out here on the farm where he could work with Sun, talk to Jo and pet Betty's ears, he could stay sober. It wasn't that hard.

Hell. He'd already asked Matthew to make the long drive down because he didn't trust himself to go into Denver and not hit a liquor store or a club. If he *had* to go to a club and spend several hours surrounded by alcohol and party people—how was he going to Just Say No? He'd wanted to crack open a fifth about three times in the last twenty minutes. And that was just talking to Matthew.

"That's why I need your help, Matthew. I don't know how to do this myself and you're the only one of us who Chadwick listens to."

"You're not just doing this for a woman?"

"She's not like that."

He needed Matthew's organization, his contacts, his ability to pacify Chadwick. Especially that.

Matthew sighed deeply. "I shouldn't."

"But you will?"

Matthew shot him a snarky look over his shoulder. "I must be nuts."

"Nope," Phillip said, unable to stop himself from grinning. He'd convinced Matthew. No matter what, that was a victory. One he knew he'd remember in the morning. "You're just a Beaumont."

Ten

Jo cleaned saddles, then Sun trashed them. The process repeated itself several times over the next three days. The only change of pace was when she paused to saddle up Betty. She'd clean a saddle again, wait for Sun to grind it into the dirt and then unsaddle Betty.

She never left Betty's saddle where Sun could get to it.

Jo felt awful and she wasn't sure why. She was not responsible for Phillip Beaumont. Never had been. She could not be the reason he drank or didn't drink. She couldn't fix him and it wasn't her responsibility to save him. Anything he did—*everything* he did—had to be a choice he made of his own free will.

However, all of that fine logic was subsumed beneath a gnawing sense of guilt. He'd been in a world of hurt and she couldn't help but feel as if she hadn't done enough. After all, she'd had a medical staff monitoring her for a couple of months. She'd moved back in with her parents and grandmother. She'd had Betty.

The fight to sobriety might have felt lonely, but she hadn't been alone.

Not like Phillip was. She didn't know what his relationship was like with the rest of his family, but she didn't think she was wrong about his brother waiting for Phillip to drink himself out of the picture.

She'd loaned him Betty for the night. And then he'd left.

She shouldn't care. Her guilt had nothing to do with the way he'd brought her coffee in the morning or kissed her hand after she made him clean saddles. It had nothing to do with how he'd looked at her as if she was the boat he could cling to in a storm.

But it did.

Jo focused on her work. What else could she do? If Phillip had given up, Sun would be sold. It hurt her to even think of that—the change would erase all the progress they'd made. But she had an obligation to make sure he was as manageable as possible, no matter who owned him.

She had a duty to herself, too—her reputation as a world-class trainer, and the reference she'd get from this job. That's where her focus had to be.

On the third day of cleaning saddles, Sun wandered over to where she'd left the jumping saddle and gave it a few half-hearted paws before he went to check on his bucket.

She didn't have any carrots. But Phillip would have.

She walked over to the saddle, dusted the hoof prints off of it, and walked away. Sun sniffed the saddle a few minutes later, but didn't trash it.

Finally, she thought. He'd gotten bored with this game they were playing. They could move on to the next phase—getting the clean saddle on the horse.

She didn't have any illusions that saddling Sun would be something she could accomplish in an afternoon. The process might take weeks—weeks she didn't know if she had.

She needed a break. For the first time, she was tired of standing in a paddock. Impatience pulled at her mind.

She gathered up the saddle and her cleaning supplies and slung them over the paddock fence. She'd leave them there so Sun would see them. Maybe Richard wouldn't mind if she borrowed one of the horses and went for a long ride. She'd love to give the Appaloosas a go.

She could call Granny. Just to check in, see how she was doing. Or she could go see a movie. Or something. Anything, really, as long as it didn't involve Beaumont Farms.

She unsaddled Betty and left the saddle next to Sun's. Jo didn't trust Sun enough yet to leave Betty alone with him, but the two animals had been co-existing better than she'd hoped. The little donkey was doing quite well in the pasture across the drive. That was another encouraging sign that should have put her in a good mood but didn't.

She was walking out of the paddock when she heard it—the sound of a car. She looked up to see a long, black limousine driving toward them.

Phillip. She glanced back at the barn, but Richard hadn't popped his head out yet.

Suddenly, Jo was nervous. One of the nice side effects of not getting involved with her clients' personal lives was that she never had to wonder how to act around them because she always acted the same—reserved. Concerned about the horses and not with their messy lives.

What if he was drunk, like he'd been the first time? It would mean he'd given up. She'd load up Betty and be gone by tonight. She wouldn't have to call Granny—she could just go home for a bit and get right with the world again.

Then she could keep doing what she'd done—traveling from ranch to farm, saving broken horses, building her business and never getting involved. She'd never have to see Phillip Beaumont again.

But what if…

The limo pulled up in front of her. Instead of the expensive Italian leather shoes and fine-cut wool trousers that he'd been wearing the first time she'd seen him get out of that limo, a pair of polished ostrich cowboy boots and artfully distressed jeans exited the vehicle.

Then Phillip stood and smiled at her over the door.

Oh God—Phillip.

Even at this distance she could see his eyes were clear and bright. His jaw was freshly shaven, his hair artfully messy.

She blinked at him as he leaned forward and thanked his driver. Then he shut the door and the limo drove off, leaving Phillip in the middle of the drive.

In addition to the jeans, he was wearing the kind of western shirt that hipsters wore—black with faint pin-stripes and a whole lot of detailed embroidery on the shoulders and cuffs. He even had a rugged-looking leather-and-silver cuff on his arm.

Her breath caught as he walked toward her. He shouldn't—couldn't—look that good. She watched for his tells—the extra-slow, extra-careful movements, the jumping eyes—but found nothing.

Phillip Beaumont strode toward her with purpose. God, he looked *so* good. Better than she remembered. Although, to be fair, he had looked like hell the last time she'd seen him. He certainly didn't look like hell at the moment. In fact, she couldn't remember him looking as confident, as capable—as *sexy*—as he did right now.

Behind her, Sun snorted. Jo heard his hoofbeats, but they weren't frantic. Sun was just trotting around. His lack of overreaction might mean he not only recognized Phillip, but was also glad to see him.

As though she was glad to see him. "You're back."

"I am." He stopped less than two feet from her—more than far enough away to be considered a respectable distance but close enough that Jo could reach out and touch him if she wanted to.

Oh, how she wanted to. The man standing before her was a hybrid of the slick, handsome playboy in commercials and the cowboy who'd worked by her side for over a week.

A man should not look this good, she decided. It wasn't fair to everyone else. It wasn't fair to her.

She forced herself to breathe regularly. No gasping allowed. "What have you been up to?"

"Did you watch *Denver This Morning* this morning?"

She gave him a look. "No."

"Or *Good Morning America* yesterday?"

"No."

"No," he said with the kind of grin that did a variety of very interesting things to her. "I didn't figure you had."

She couldn't help herself. She leaned forward and took a deep breath, just as Granny had done once to her. Coffee, subtly blended with bay rum spice. Not a hint of alcohol on him.

"I've had a lot of coffee in the last five and a half days." He smelled warm and clean and tempting. Oh so tempting. "It's a good place to start, I've heard."

"As good as any," she agreed. Why was breathing so hard right now? She shouldn't care that he'd been sober for five days. She shouldn't care that he'd come back to the farm looking better than any man had a right to look.

"I hired a sober coach," he went on. "Big guy named Fred. He'll help me stay on the straight and narrow. I'm meeting with him tomorrow morning and he'll be accompanying me to all my required club appearances."

"You did...*what?*" She couldn't have heard him right.

"Sober coach. To help me stay sober. So I can save my farm." He lowered his head to look at her. "I wanted to thank you."

She blinked at him. Why was he telling her this? "For what?"

Before he could answer, Betty wandered over and leaned into his leg, demanding to be petted. "Hey, girl," he said in a bemused tone as he rubbed her head. "Been keeping an eye on Jo for me?"

He'd been thinking of her. "She missed you," Jo managed to say.

Phillip notched an eyebrow at her. Yeah, she wasn't fooling him any. How could she hope to fool herself?

You gave up men when you gave up drinking, she reminded herself as he pulled a device out of his back pocket. *You don't get to have this. Him.*

Phillip tapped on the screen a few times. "Here," he said, handing it to her.

The sun chose that moment to break through the clouds. The glare off the screen made it impossible to watch what he'd called up, but she heard a perky voice say, "...with us this morning is the handsome face of the Beaumont Brewery, Phillip Beaumont himself."

"I can't see," she told him.

"You need to get out of the sun."

She glanced back at her trailer. Suddenly, the distance of a couple hundred feet felt way too close and also too far away at the same time. "We could go to my trailer."

The moment she said it, she knew she'd meant something other than to just watch a video.

She turned her head back to Phillip. Her mind was swimming. Fifteen minutes ago, she'd written him off as a drunk who wasn't interested in saving himself. But now?

Their eyes met and a spark of something so intense it almost wasn't recognizable passed between them. She recognized it anyway. Sheer, unadulterated lust coursed through her, suddenly as vital as the blood that pounded through her heart.

This was the moment.

She could invite Phillip back to her trailer and pin him against the wall and kiss him as a reward for having had nothing but coffee for almost a week and no one would ever know.

Except she would.

And so would he.

"We could," Phillip said, his voice dropping down to something that would have been a whisper if the tone hadn't been so deep. "If that's what you want."

She wanted. She wanted the Phillip who wasn't afraid to grab a hay bale or clean a saddle, the Phillip who knew how to harness and drive a team. The Phillip who made her blush.

She wanted to kiss him.

Unable to come up with any words at all, she simply turned and walked to her trailer.

She opened the door and stepped up. But she didn't make a move toward the bed. She stopped at the top of the steps and turned.

Phillip stopped, too—one foot on the lowest step. He wasn't inside, but he wasn't out either.

"Here," he said, leaning forward to tap the screen a few more times. "Watch."

The video restarted. "Welcome back to *Good Morning, America*," a perky woman who looked vaguely familiar beamed into the camera. "With us this morning is the handsome face of the Beaumont Brewery, Phillip Beaumont himself."

The camera panned to Phillip sitting on a couch. His leg was crossed and his hands rested on his shin. He seemed quite comfortable on camera. He looked so good in his fancy western shirt—different than the one he was wearing now—and boots that were probably eel. He grinned at the perky woman—the same grin he'd given Jo the first time they'd met.

"The Beaumont Brewery is home to the world-famous Beaumont Percherons," the woman went on. "But there could be some changes underway and Phillip is here today with the details. Phillip?"

Phillip turned his attention to the camera. There he was, the sophisticated man-about-town. "Thanks, Julie. The Percherons have been a part of the Beaumont Brewery since 1868."

The screen cut away to a black-and-white commercial with the Percherons leading a wagon of beer. Phillip's voice over explained the history of the Brewery's Percheron team from the Colorado Territory to the present as decades of commercials played.

Besides the quality of the video, very little changed across the years. The horses were all nearly identical, the wagon the same—years of Beaumont Percherons anchoring the company to the public consciousness.

The camera refocused on Phillip and the woman. "Those are some classic commercials," the woman announced.

"They are," Phillip agreed. "But now the Beaumont Brewery is trying to decide whether to branch out from the Percherons or stick with tradition. So we've set up a poll for people to vote—should Beaumont Brewery keep the Percherons or not?"

"Fascinating," the woman said as she nodded eagerly. "How can people vote?"

"Visit the Facebook page we've set up for the poll," Phillip said as the web address popped up at the bottom of the screen. "We encourage people to leave a comment telling us what the Percherons mean to them."

Phillip and the woman engaged in a little more light banter before the segment ended.

Jo blinked at the screen. "You did that?"

"I'd show you the one from *Denver This Morning*, but it was basically the same thing," he said. Then he set his other foot on the step.

"We?" Because that interview had been a lot of *we*—*we* set up the poll, *we* made a Facebook page.

"My brother Matthew helped me," he corrected. "But they didn't know that Chadwick hadn't exactly signed off on this particular line of publicity." He smiled the wicked smile of a man who does whatever he wants and gets away with it. "We've already had over sixty thousand votes to keep the Percherons and four thousand comments in less than forty-eight hours. I dare Chadwick to ignore that—and I doubt the new Brewery owners will be able to ignore it, either."

"You," she whispered, staring at the screen as if it held all the answers.

He wasn't going to give up on Sun or the Percherons. Or himself. He wasn't going down without a damned good fight.

He lifted her hat off her head and set it in the seat next to the door. He wasn't touching her, not really, but licking flames danced over her skin, setting her on fire. "I did a lot of thinking that night," he said, low and close. So close she could kiss him. "About who I was and what I wanted. Who I wanted to be."

"I know you didn't sleep," she admitted. "Neither did I."

"I decided I needed to make some changes, so I called my cleaning service the next morning," he went on, brushing his fingertips over her cheek and pushing her hair back. "I had them get rid of all the alcohol in my apartment in the city. I also told Richard to get everything out of the house and give it to the hands. I talked to Matthew and hired a sober coach."

"You did all that?" Amazing, yes—but why? Because

no matter how impressive of a step it was, she couldn't be the reason. "Did you do this for me?"

He climbed the second step. The door swung shut behind him, closing them off from the rest of the world. They were the same height now, close enough she could feel the heat from his chest radiating through his shirt. He brought his other hand up, cupping her face. "If you were any other woman in the world, I'd say yes." He searched her eyes. "But…"

"But?" It was the most important *but* she'd ever said.

"But," he went on, a small, soft grin taking hold of his lips, "I didn't. Not really."

"Who did you do it for?"

"I did it for Sun and Marge and Homer and Snowflake and all the horses. I even did it for Richard, the old goat, because he's a good farm manager and he's too damn old to be unemployed."

"Yeah?" She couldn't help herself. She dropped the device on top of her hat and slid her arms around his waist. He was solid and warm and quite possibly the best thing she'd ever held.

"I did it for me," he told her.

It should have sounded like a selfish announcement from one of the most selfish men in the world, but it didn't. His voice was low and steady and he looked at her with such heated fervor that she knew the touch of his lips would scorch her and there'd be no turning back.

"Because I couldn't live with myself if I let it go."

"Oh," was all she could say. It seemed inadequate. So she surrendered to the pull he had on her and kissed him. She couldn't fight her attraction to him any longer and she was tired of trying.

It was a simple touch of her lips to his, but he sighed into her with such contentment that it demolished her reserves. *Skin on skin.* Desire burned through her. Her nipples went tight—so tight it almost hurt. Only his touch could ease the pain.

She was kissing Phillip Beaumont, really kissing him. She tilted her head for better access. He responded by opening his mouth for her. When she swept her tongue in to touch his, he groaned, "Jo." Then he kissed her back.

Any sense she had left evaporated. She ran her fingers up his back, feeling each muscle before she laced her fingers through his hair. Everything about her felt…odd. Different. Warm and hot and shivery all at the same time.

She wanted to see the body that was doing things to her—pooling heat low in her belly that demanded attention *right now*. The weight between her legs got so heavy so fast that she was suddenly having trouble standing.

And thinking? Yeah, that wasn't happening either. All she could think was how long it'd been. Years. Over a decade she'd denied that she needed this—to feel a man's arms around hers, to feel desirable.

She grabbed the front of his shirt. Snaps, not buttons. *Done*. The shirt gave and Phillip's chest was laid bare for her.

She had to look—had to—so she broke the kiss and let her fingertips trace the outline of his chest.

Carved of stone, that's what his muscles were. Smooth and hard but warm—almost hot to the touch. Or maybe that was just her. "Wow," she breathed as she traced his six-pack.

"Mmm," he said, pushing the hair away from the left side of her neck—the smooth side—and…and…

Years of pent-up sexual frustration unleashed themselves on her when he bit down on the space between her shoulder and her neck. Her hips tilted toward him, desperate for a release of the tightness that felt like a rubber band about to snap back on her. "*Phillip.*"

"Too hard?" He kissed the spot he'd bitten. It was all the more tender compared to his bite.

This was it—the last possible moment she could back away from the edge before she went spiraling out of control.

Except she didn't want to back away. She wanted to throw herself forward without a look back.

"No," she said, grabbing at his belt buckle. The damned thing was far more complicated than the shirt had been. "Not hard enough."

He growled against her skin. "Bed?"

"Bed." Although she didn't exactly care at this moment where they wound up. Just so long as he kept doing what he was doing.

Then, to her surprise, Phillip picked her up. He held her against his chest as he mounted the last step. One arm around her waist, one under her bottom. The hand under her bottom squeezed her hard, making her squirm.

"You like it a little hard?" he asked.

"A little rough." Or, at least, she thought she did. A wave of insecurity almost froze her. "It's been so long...." Not only that, but she'd never done this with the scars. Even though the blinds were down, enough daylight suffused the bedroom that there was no way to hide.

He set her down and cupped her face again. "Then we better make sure it's worth the wait." As he kissed her, he unsnapped her shirt. "You about killed me the other night," he murmured against her skin before biting her shoulder as he pushed off her shirt.

She swallowed. "I did?"

The shirt hit the ground and then his fingers were tracing the swells of her breasts, barely contained by her bra. "Just a glimpse of you...." Then his mouth was moving lower as his hands went around her back. Over her scars. "I wanted a taste."

The bra gave and mercifully he brought his hands up to cup her breasts again. "Amazing," he whispered as his tongue lapped against her rock-hard nipple. "Simply amazing."

"I…"

He scraped his teeth down the side of her breast as he pulled her nipple into his mouth. "Yes?"

There was no mistaking the bulge in his jeans. "More," she gasped as he sucked hard.

"I love a woman who knows what she wants," he replied, smoothly undoing her belt and then her jeans.

He sat her down on the bed, where she kicked off her boots and jeans. Then she was in nothing but her panties.

Her pulse was racing so hard that she was having trouble focusing.

Which, admittedly, became a whole lot easier when Phillip undid his stubborn belt and shucked his jeans. His erection strained against the boxer-briefs he wore—red, of course—and those were gone, too.

Jo began to breathe so fast she was in danger of panting. She felt as if she should say something, but the problem was, she didn't know what. She was no shy, retiring virgin—but she had been celibate for the last decade.

She didn't know what she was doing.

Phillip stepped toward her. Jo sat up. Maybe he expected her to start with a little oral? Although—honestly—there wasn't much that was "little" about it.

He was, for lack of a better word, *huge*. She took him in hand, her fingers barely meeting as she encircled him. Once, twice, she moved her hand up and down.

"Jo," he groaned as his hands tangled in her hair.

When she leaned forward to take him in her mouth, he stopped her. "Wait."

"Wait?"

He pushed her back with enough force that she had to

lean on her elbows. She watched as he took a deep breath—a man struggling to remain in control. Then he opened his eyes—the green much darker with desire. "Saving the farm," he said, the strain in his voice unmistakable, "isn't about you."

Phillip crouched down to the ground and pulled a condom out of his back pocket. "But this," he said, dropping the condom on the bed next to her, "this *is.*"

Before she could process that, he'd kneeled between her legs and was pulling her panties down. "It's really been ten years?"

She couldn't even talk as his fingertips slid down her thighs, over her knees, down her ankles. She bit her lip and tried to nod, but her head felt as if it was in danger of floating away.

His hands skimmed up her calves, flushing her with heat as he sat on his heels and looked her over. For a moment, she panicked. He was used to other kinds of women—women with perfect bodies and flat stomachs and smooth, soft skin. She hadn't even shaved her bikini line recently. She hadn't planned on things getting this far, this fast.

For a horrific moment, she wished she had a drink. A shot of liquid courage to help her get out of her own head and into the perfect man between her legs. And the moment she thought that, she almost told him to stop.

Like alcohol, men were a drug she'd already quit once.

Phillip leaned down and kissed…her knee. "Do you want to remember this?"

"What?"

He kissed her other knee. "You said you didn't remember the sex before. Didn't remember if you wanted it or not."

Good to know he'd been paying attention and all, but she was pretty sure this wasn't a normal seduction.

He shifted to place a kiss on her hip bone. It shouldn't have felt good—just a regular old hip bone—but the tender way he was touching her focused her thoughts. Where would he kiss her next?

"Well?" Another kiss on the top of her thigh.

"I want to remember," she told him, knowing it was the truth. "I want to remember *you*."

Eleven

Yes. "That's what I want, too."

He leaned forward, letting his erection brush against her as he kissed the spot where he'd lost his head and bit down earlier. "Do you still want it a little rough? Or a little gentle?" Then he flicked his tongue over her earlobe.

She squirmed underneath him, which about drove him insane. "Both? Is that even an answer?" She tried to laugh it off as a joke, but he heard something else.

She was nervous. Well, he couldn't blame her. Ten years was a long time.

He grabbed her hands and pinned her down. Much more of her body moving under his and they wouldn't even make it to the memorable sex.

His arms began to shake under the strain of not plunging into her warm body. But he had to do this right for her.

"Both it is." Soft and tough—just like she was.

He bit down on the spot that had nearly broken her earlier. She sucked in a hot breath against his ear, her hips thrusting up against him. *Yes*, he thought again.

He moved to the other side—the side where she wore her scars like tattoos. She tried to tilt her head to hide herself but he had her pinned.

He kissed down her shoulder until he switched to her breast—full and heavy.

He licked her nipple, blowing air on the wet skin to see it tighten up. Her hips shimmied beneath his. Not yet. Too soon. He had to kneel back to break the contact.

He kissed the space between her breasts and then used his teeth to leave a mark on the inside of the left one. She sucked air again as her body strained against his hands. "Okay?" he asked, just to be sure.

"Yes." She nodded, but her eyes were closed.

"Then look at me," he ordered. When she didn't immediately open her eyes, he bit her again, his teeth skimming her nipple. "*Jo*. Look at what I'm doing to you."

Then he fastened onto her nipple and sucked hard until her eyes flew open. There—the anxiety that had lurked there earlier was gone, leaving nothing but need and want in its place.

He let his teeth scrape over her, putting a hint of pressure on her skin. Not enough to hurt her, but more than enough that she wouldn't forget this.

"Oh—Phillip," she gasped out, tilting her hips up—begging for his touch.

He didn't let go of her hands as he moved his mouth lower and lower. He pulled her with him until she was nearly sitting up. No way he was going to let her lie back.

"Keep your eyes open," he told her before he pressed a kiss against her sex.

"Why," she ground out through clenched teeth as he licked her, "why do you get to do this to me and I didn't get to do it to you?"

It was a fair enough question. "You've been a very good girl," he told her, keeping his mouth against her so she'd feel his voice more than she heard it. It worked, given the way she bucked against him, her body asking for more even if her mouth couldn't. He looked up the length of her body—she was watching him. *Good.* "You deserve a reward."

He filled his mouth with her, savoring her taste the way he'd savor a fine wine. Nothing was clouded by the haze of a wild night. This was just him and her and *nothing* in between them.

He was not gentle. It paid off. After only a few agonizing minutes of teasing her, Jo's back arched off the bed. She made a high-pitched noise in the back of her throat before collapsing back against the bed, panting hard.

He kissed her inner thigh, then turned his head and bit the other one. His dick throbbed, but in a good way. "Memorable?"

"Unforgettable," she said and this time, there was no hesitation in her voice at all. Nothing but a dreamy tone that spoke volumes about satisfaction.

"Good." He swallowed, the taste of her desire still on his lips. "Now roll over."

Jo froze. "What?"

She couldn't roll over. She absolutely could not have sex with a man—especially a man as physically perfect at Phillip Beaumont—where the only thing he could see would be the burn marks on her back.

He covered her body with his, the weight of his erection pressing hard against her. Her mind was in a state of confusion, but her body? Nothing confused there. That first orgasm had primed her pump, just as she knew it would. She needed more. She couldn't get enough of him.

He leaned over her and placed his teeth against her

neck. His hips flexed, putting him right against her. "Do you want this?"

She nodded.

He moved to the other side of her neck. The side with the scars that usually hid behind the collar of her shirts and her hair.

But she couldn't hide from him now. He wouldn't allow it.

"You can have it if you roll over," he whispered against her skin. He flexed again, his tip pushing against her. "Roll over for me, Jo. Don't hide who you really are."

"But I'm—it's—so ugly."

"Not to me." He let go of her and propped himself up on his hands so he could look her fully in the eyes. "It wasn't ugly when you stripped for me the other night. It was real and honest and true. That's what you are to me, Jo—the truth. No one else gives me a hard time like you do. No one else expects me to do anything—*be* anything. But you expect better of me. You make me want to be a better man."

They weren't the words of seduction, not even close. But that didn't change the fact that it was the sweetest thing anyone had ever said to her.

She took his face in her hands. "I can't be the reason." She wasn't fooling herself. When Sun was manageable, she and Betty would be gone and Phillip would be on his own again. The changes in his life couldn't be because of her.

That wicked grin would be her undoing. "You can be one of them. And a far more beautiful one than Richard's wrinkly old mug."

He leaned down to kiss her. The taste of coffee gone now; nothing but her and him mingled together. Her skin burned in the best possible way where he'd left marks on her body—pulling her into the here and now by brute force.

He flexed again, insistent in his need. "Let me see you, Jo. All of you."

She rolled, careful not to kick him.

Then she was exposed. Totally, utterly exposed to him. It left her feeling raw.

She didn't realize how tense she was until the first touch came. When his hands traced her shoulders, she jumped. "Sorry."

"Don't be." He smoothed her hair away and kissed the scar. His hands moved over her ribs, his fingertips tracing the sides of her breasts.

Then he was moving lower—kissing the surgical scars that ran alongside where her back had been broken. She'd been so broken.

She didn't feel broken right now. How could she, with Phillip lavishing such tender caresses on her?

He kissed the base of her back, just above her bottom. "You are so beautiful," he groaned—and then bit one of her cheeks.

Jo started against the bed. It felt good. It felt…as though she was alive. She grabbed the sheets and closed her eyes, letting her skin feel what she couldn't see—Phillip. She memorized every touch.

His hand grabbed her other cheek and squeezed, then a finger slipped inside of her. She clenched down. "More." She needed all of him.

His warmth left her. She turned her head to see him ripping open the condom wrapper, then rolling on the protection. Then he grabbed her hips, pulling her back to him with anything but gentleness.

Both. She'd asked for both because she didn't know what she wanted, not anymore. Just him.

Make it worth ten years of waiting, she thought.

He touched her again. "You're so ready for me." His tone was almost reverent. Then he was against her and, with a thrust, buried inside of her.

Jo's back arched as she groaned. "Oh, yes, *please*."

But he didn't. He stopped. The seconds dragged on for years before he grabbed her by the hips again, tilting her backside up. Then he grabbed her hair and wrapped it around his fist. "If this pulls at your back, you tell me, okay?"

Then he tugged her head back. Her neck lengthened and suddenly, his mouth was on her throat, biting at just the right spot.

Then he thrust. All Jo could do was groan at the wonderful agony of it all.

"Okay?"

"More." He tugged at her hair, popping her head up. "More, *please*."

He fell into a rhythm—long, steady strokes punctuated only by his teeth against her skin. Every bite, every thrust kept her in the here and now. Just her and Phillip.

It was freeing. She was free.

Jo came with a cry that she muffled against the mattress. Leaning back, Phillip let go of her hair and dug his fingertips into the flesh of her bottom, thrusting harder and harder until he let go with a low roar of pure satisfaction. Then he fell forward on her.

"Jo," he whispered in her ear in a voice that made him sound vulnerable.

She rolled again—not to hide her skin from him, but to face him.

Phillip smoothed her hair away from her cheeks and kissed her softly. "Beautiful," he sighed against her lips before he pulled her into a strong hug.

This was so much better than waking up with a sense of horror at feeling used and alone and knowing it was her own damned fault.

Her skin was still warm from Phillip's touch, her body weak from the orgasms. She wouldn't forget this. She wouldn't forget him.

And now that she had this moment, how was she supposed to not want it more? Already, she wanted him again.

Oh, no.

She couldn't believe she'd done this. She'd thrown away ten years of sticking to the straight and narrow and for what? For thirty minutes of sweet, heady freedom with Phillip Beaumont, a world-renowned womanizer with all of five days of sobriety under his belt?

How could she have been so stupid?

Then his phone rang.

Twelve

"Is that…the Darth Vader theme music?"

Phillip tensed at the sound of Chadwick's ring tone. "The 'Imperial March,' yes."

He pulled Jo into his arms and kissed her forehead. He didn't want to get up. He wanted to stay here and explore Jo some more. Yeah, he'd wanted to make that memorable but the truth was, he wasn't going to forget her.

It was a weird feeling to realize that he couldn't remember the face, much less the name, of the last woman he'd been with. It all ran together.

Everything about Jo stood out. The way her body had closed around his, the way she'd responded to his touch, his commands—he wanted to do that again, just to make sure it hadn't been some one-off fluke.

But Chadwick was calling. He'd gotten wind of what Phillip had been up to.

This was about to get ugly.

He forced himself to let go of her and sat up. "I need to leave."

"Oh."

He didn't like her quiet note. But before he could say anything else, his phone started singing again. He grabbed his pants off the floor.

She tried to slip past him, but he hadn't forgotten that vulnerable *Oh.* "Tonight," he said as he grabbed her arm.

"Tonight?" Anything vulnerable about her was gone and the tough cowgirl was back in place.

"Have dinner with me." His phone stopped marching, only to pick up the beat two seconds later. "Come up to the house."

She tilted her head toward him and waited. The power had shifted between them. She'd given him control over the sex, but she'd taken that back now.

"Please," he added as he curled his arm around her waist. He put his lips against the curve of her neck and whispered, "Please," against her skin.

She pulled away from him. "No."

Then she was gone, striding down the hall and out the trailer before he could process what she'd just said. *No?*

He stared at the empty hallway, then the bed they'd only just vacated. What happened? One minute they were having electric sex—her pleading for more, for the release he knew she couldn't have been faking. The best sex he could remember. And the next, she was *done* with him?

He started after her, but his damned phone began to march again. *Son of a...*

"What?" he demanded as he slammed the trailer door shut after him. Jo already had Betty and was shutting the paddock gate behind them both.

She couldn't have been clearer—she didn't want to talk to him.

"Have you lost your mind?" Chadwick thundered on the other end.

"And hello to you, too," Phillip said as he tried to figure out where he'd gone wrong. She'd wanted it both soft and rough. Hadn't he delivered?

"You are single-handedly jeopardizing this *entire* deal," Chadwick yelled in his ear. "Even by your standards, you've screwed this up."

"I've done nothing of the sort," Phillip replied, forcing himself to remain calm. Mostly because he knew he wouldn't win a shouting match with his older brother, but also because he knew it'd drive the jerk crazy. "I've merely reminded the future owners of our brewery that we mean more to our vast customer base than just a nice, cold beer."

Jo stood with her back to him as she haltered Betty. Sun was aware of him, though. The horse was making short strides back and forth in front of her, his head never pointing away from where Phillip was pacing.

"...pissed off Harper and the entire board," Chadwick was yelling. "Do you know what that man will do to us if this deal falls through?"

"To hell with Harper," Phillip said, only half paying attention. Maybe he should have asked Jo if he could come back to her trailer instead of inviting her up to the house? "I can't stand the guy. And he hates us."

"I always thought you had a brain somewhere in that head of yours and that you *chose* not to use it," Chadwick fumed. "I can see now that I was wrong. For your information, Phillip, Harper will sue us into last *century*. And any hope that you're keeping the farm with this PR gambit will go down the drain in legal fees."

"Oh," Phillip said, Chadwick's words registering for the first time. "I hadn't thought about that."

"What a surprise—you didn't think something through. You *never* think things through, do you?" Chadwick made a noise of disgust in the back of his throat. "All you care about is where the next party is."

"That's not true," Phillip snapped. His head began to throb. This would be the time in his conversation with Chadwick where he'd normally tuck the phone under his chin and start opening cabinets to see if he had any whiskey. He hated it when his older brother talked down to him.

Even though Phillip knew he wasn't going to drink, the habit had him looking around for a cabinet.

Damn, this was going to be harder than he thought.

"Isn't it?" Chadwick's tone made it clear that he was sneering. "The next party, the next drink, the next woman. You've never cared for anything else in your entire, selfish life."

Phillip's pride stung, mostly because it was a somewhat accurate statement. But not entirely, and he clung to that *not* with everything he had.

If Chadwick wanted to hit below the belt, fine. Phillip would just hit right back. "You know who you sound like right now?" he said in his most calm voice, "Dad."

There was a hideous screeching noise and then the call ended. If he had to guess, Phillip would say Chadwick had thrown his phone at a wall. Good. That meant the asshole wouldn't be calling back anytime soon.

He glared at the phone, then the silent woman who, not twenty feet away from him, was leading Betty around the paddock. She might as well have been on a different continent. Any good buzz he'd had earlier from his media coup and seduction of Jo was dead.

He'd had a plan—show Chadwick and the new Brewery owners that the Percherons were too valuable to auction off.

That plan wasn't dead, he realized. He'd just finished Phase One. Now he needed to start Phase Two—getting control of this farm away from Chadwick.

Which meant he needed a new plan.

He looked at the paddock again. The cold shoulder from Jo was about to give him frostbite.

One-night stands were his specialty. He loved them when they were there, forgot about them when they were gone. So what if Jo was ignoring him? No big deal, right? He'd had his fun, just as he always did. Now was as good a time as any to move on.

But he didn't want to move on.

It must be the chase. She was exceptionally hard to get—that had to be what still called to him.

Fine. She wanted to be chased? He'd chase.

Time for Phase Two.

Thirteen

Jo needed to go in. A breeze had picked up as dusk approached and, given the clouds that were scuttling across the spring sky, they were in for some rain. She hoped it was a gentle rain and not Mother Nature throwing a fit, but she wasn't going to hold her breath.

Besides, her legs ached. Okay, so it wasn't the standing and walking that had them aching. That was more to do with the *unusual* strain of the afternoon.

She shoved back that thought and focused on the tasks at hand. If it was going to rain, she wanted to brush Betty before the donkey could track any more dirt into the trailer. And Sun—a gentle rain wouldn't kill the horse, but a storm with crashing thunder and lightning might push him over the edge. She couldn't risk him trying to bust through the fences. She needed to get him haltered and into the barn.

She needed not to get killed doing it. There wasn't anyone else around at this point—everyone else had driven off about half an hour ago.

She was not going to ask Phillip for help. She didn't need it. She wouldn't need *him*.

Jo was so focused on her work that the effort was physically exhausting. But it was still better than thinking about what she'd just done. With Phillip.

So she didn't think about it. She thought about the horse.

Sun was, by all reasonable measurements, quite calm. She haltered Betty again and led the patient donkey around the paddock again. This time, she walked within five feet of Sun. The horse didn't skitter away.

No, she was not thinking about the way Phillip had picked her up and carried her back to bed. She was also not thinking about the way he'd made her watch as he went down on her. And she was certainly not thinking about the way every molecule in her body had been pulling her into his arms when he'd whispered "Please" against her skin.

How she'd wanted to say *yes*. Just…let herself be at his beck and call. Be in his bed when he wanted, how he wanted. Let him mark her skin and fill her body and make her come so hard. It'd be easy—for as long as she was here, she could have him.

He could have her.

But then what? She was going to throw herself at him—because, God, she *wanted* to throw herself at him—and then quit him cold turkey in a week, or two weeks or however long she had left to train Sun?

And if she went to his house, went to his bed—word would get out. People would notice. People would *talk*. Her reputation as a professional horse trainer who could take on the toughest cases would be shot to hell and back. People would think she'd gotten this job because she was sleeping with Phillip.

She knew what kind of man he was. He'd move on, just as he always did.

Just as she used to do. One man was the same as another, after all.

But he'd made her remember what she liked about men in the first place. The warm bodies, soft and hard at the same time. The way orgasms felt different in someone else's arms compared to when she did them herself. The feeling, for a fleeting moment, of being complete.

That was the part she'd blindly run after. She'd always confused being *wanted* with being *had*, though. But now she knew. Wanting and having were not the same.

She'd wanted Phillip. Now she'd had him. But, unlike all those men from long ago, she wanted him again. Not just *a* man, but Phillip.

God, she was so mad at herself. She knew she couldn't have him and just let him go any more than she could have one drink and not have any more. She *knew* that. What had she been thinking?

That was the problem. She didn't know what to think anymore.

So she un-haltered Betty. And re-haltered her. Again.

This time, she walked up to Sun and stopped right in front of him. The horse's head popped up and he stared at her, his ears pointed at her as he chewed grass.

This was good. She wished she felt more excited about the victory.

"See?" she said in a soft voice. Sun's head jerked back, but he didn't bolt. "It's not so bad. Betty doesn't mind it, do you girl?"

She rubbed Betty's head between her ears. *It's not so bad*, she silently repeated to herself. She'd had Phillip once. She could back away from the brink of self-destruction again. She'd already said no to him a second time, right? Right. *Not so bad.*

Out of the corner of her eye, she saw movement. Then, unexpectedly, Sun's nose touched Betty's. It was a brief thing, lasting only two seconds, tops. Then Sun backed up and trotted off, looking as if he'd just won the horse lottery.

Jo grinned at his retreating form as she un-haltered Betty. So her mental state was all out of whack. The horse, however, was doing fine and dandy. She watched as Betty trotted after Sun. It looked like a little sister chasing after her big brother. Jo could almost hear Betty saying, "*Wait for me!*"

Jo walked back over to the gate and picked up Sun's halter and lead rope. Maybe… "Betty," she called. "Come on."

Betty exhaled in what was clearly donkey frustration. She only had so much patience for non-stop haltering. But after a moment, she plodded toward Jo.

Sun followed.

Jo moved slowly, demonstrating on Betty how the halter went over the nose and then the ears, then how the lead rope clipped on. She knew he'd been haltered before, but a refresher never hurt anyone.

She held the halter up for Sun to sniff just as a distant rumble echoed from the clouds. Sun whipped his head around, trying to find the source of the noise—then he took off at a jumpy trot. Crap. This whole process needed to happen sooner rather than later. She didn't want to spend a night standing in a downpour just to make sure Sun didn't accidentally kill himself.

Just then, Sun's ears whipped back and he blew past her to rush to the edge of the paddock. Seconds later, she heard it, too—the sound of whistling.

Yes, she was mad at herself and yes, she knew that it wasn't healthy to take her anger out on anyone else but *damn* it was tempting to light into Phillip. Everything had been going fine until he'd arrived on the farm. She'd been a well-respected horse trainer that never, ever gave in to temptation, no matter how long or lonely the nights were.

She wanted to go back to being in control, removed from the messy lives of her clients.

She also wanted to stomp over to that gate, throw it open and demand to know what the hell he was thinking, but she didn't get that far.

Phillip came forward, looking at the halter in her hands. "Any luck?"

Then he had the damned nerve to wink at her.

She wanted to tell him to shove his luck where the sun didn't shine but she didn't. "I *was* making progress. A storm's coming in. I need to move him to the barn without setting him off again."

Phillip looked at her with such intensity that it made her sweat. "I know what he needs," he replied in a voice that was too casual to be anything *but* a double entendre.

She glared at him. She was not going to lose her head again. She was not going to give in to her addictions. One and done. That was final.

He reached into his shirt pocket and pulled out a small baggie of carrots. "Oh," she said, feeling stupid. "Okay."

Phillip opened the gate and walked in. He took out a carrot and stood remarkably still, the carrot held out on the flat of his palm.

Betty came up to him, her lead rope trailing behind her as she snuffled for the treat. "Go ahead," Jo said when Phillip looked to her for approval.

Sun looped around the paddock a few times, each circle tightening on where Phillip stood, another carrot at the ready. This wasn't how she wanted to do this. They were forcing something that she normally would have worked on for a week, maybe more.

But the sky was starting to roil as the clouds built and moved. So she stood next to Phillip, ready to halter a horse.

They waited. For once, Phillip had all the patience in the

paddock. Jo was the one who kept glancing at the menacing clouds as if she could keep them at bay by sheer will.

"Come on, Sun," Phillip said in a low voice that sent a tremor down Jo's back. "It'll be okay, you'll see."

Miraculously, Sun came. Head down, he walked toward them as if he agreed to be haltered every day.

Jo held her breath as the horse sniffed the carrot in the man's palm. Then Sun's big teeth scraped the carrot off Phillip's hand.

"Good, huh?" Phillip said, lifting his hand to rub Sun's nose. "I have more if you let Jo put the halter on you."

Sun shook his head and walked away. But he didn't go far.

A few days ago, Phillip might have whined about how long this was taking. But not today. He merely got another carrot out and waited.

Betty leaned against his legs, so he broke the carrot in half and gave her the smaller part. That got Sun's attention, fast. He came back over to Phillip.

"Carrots," Phillip said, letting Sun take the remaining half, "are *that* good, aren't they?"

He started to fish out another carrot—and Sun was waiting for it—but Jo stopped him. "Let me try to get the halter on, then give him another one if he cooperates."

Sun gave her a baleful look. Clearly, he was too smart for his own good.

"You heard the lady," Phillip said in a teasing tone to his horse. "No more without the halter."

Sun shook his head again. Thunder rumbled again, closer this time.

"You don't want to spend the night in the rain, do you?" Sun blew snot on the ground. "No," Phillip went on, "I didn't think so." He held out another carrot so Sun could smell it.

Jo stepped forward as quickly as she could and slipped

the halter over Sun's nose. He shook her off and reached for the carrot, but Phillip pulled back. "No halter, no carrot."

Sun dropped his head in resignation. Jo slipped the lead rope over his neck and handed the ends to Phillip. Then she leaned forward and slipped the halter over his nose, then over his ears. She clipped the throat latch.

Victory. She knew it, Phillip knew it—hell, even Betty seemed to know it. She clipped the lead rope on the halter. Phillip gave Sun another carrot.

"Now we have to get him to the barn," she said. "Can you lead him?"

Phillip gave her the kind of smile that didn't so much chip away at her defenses as blow them up. Nope. Not working on her today. Or any other day.

She was not that girl anymore. She would not throw herself at a man. Not even Phillip Beaumont.

"I can honestly say I've done this before. Plus," he added with that grin, "I'm the one with the carrots."

She steeled her resolve. Sun hadn't been indoors in almost two weeks. This could go south on them. Maybe she should leave Betty in the stall next to Sun for the night? It couldn't hurt. "Fine. Betty and I will lead the way."

Why did she have a sinking feeling that things were about to get interesting?

Phillip had a death grip on the lead rope. The odds that Sun would freak out were maybe 50/50. He couldn't do anything about bucking except stay out of the way, but if Sun tried to bolt, he'd have to spin the horse in a small, tight circle before he could build up a head of steam. And if he reared…

Damn, Phillip wished he had on some gloves. If Sun reared, Phillip just might get rope burn on both palms. He tightened his grip.

He followed Jo and Betty into the barn. The lights came

on overhead, which made Sun start, but he didn't bolt. Jo
led her donkey past Sun's stall and then paused. "This stall
is empty," she said in a gentle voice. "I'll put Betty in."

"Okay." The situation made him nervous. Leading a
mostly-calm Sun down a wide hallway was one thing.
Being in a stall with him was a whole different thing.

"Easy does it," Jo said. For the first time since she'd
walked away from him that afternoon, he heard something
soft in her voice.

Phillip nodded as he walked into the stall with Sun.
Then Jo was standing next to him, unclipping the throat
latch and sliding the halter from Sun's head.

The three of them stood there for a moment, humans
and horse, wondering if they'd just accomplished that without shouting, ropes or guns. Sun shook his head and pawed
at the ground, but didn't freak out. Hell, he didn't do anything even remotely Sun-like. He just stood there.

"Carrot?" Jo said in her quiet voice.

"Carrot," Phillip agreed, fishing the rest out of his
pocket and holding them out to the horse.

His horse.

The wind gusted. He gave Jo a sideways smile that was
absolutely not working. "It's going to storm."

"I know."

"We're under a tornado watch until eleven p.m.," he
told her. "You should come up to the house—the trailer
may not be safe."

Of all the sneaky, underhanded things… "I'll sleep in
the barn with the horses."

"*Jo.*" He was forced to shout as the wind gusted up.
"Come to the house, damn it. This isn't about seduction,
this is about safety."

She hesitated. "I'm not sleeping with you tonight."

He stared at her. "First off, I have a fully stocked guest room. Second off…" He stepped toward her. "I'm sorry."

"For what?"

He ducked his head, looking sheepish. "Well, that's part of the problem. I'm not sure for what. But I've clearly done something you didn't like and it's put me in an odd position."

She stared at him as he studied the tips of his toes. Was this actual sincerity? "What position is that?"

"I want to make it up to you, but I don't have the first idea how. I mean, normally, I wouldn't even care if I'd been a jerk and if I did, I'd throw some roses or diamonds at the problem and be done with it. But I know that won't work. And I don't want to be done with it. With you."

Oh, God. This was sincerity. She considered bolting from the barn, but there was no guarantee he wouldn't follow her. "What do you want from me, Phillip?"

"I want…" He turned away as he ran his hands through his hair. "I want to understand what it is about you that makes me want to do…things. Stay home on the farm. Stay sober. Not—" He paused.

Jo leaned forward, suddenly very interested in that *not*. "Yes?"

He let out a short, sharp laugh. "Is it always this hard?"

"No. Sometimes it's harder." Although, frankly, this was pretty damned hard. She hadn't been faced with this level of emotion—involvement—in so long. She didn't know what to do.

It'd be easy to think he was feeding her a line of bull.

She watched as the muscles in his jaw twitched. He really thought he'd screwed up. Damn.

"If I say it's not you, it's me—will you laugh?" she asked.

That got her a rueful grin. "I haven't heard that line in a long time."

"I had given up men, remember?" She wanted to touch him, but she didn't want to. Life was so much simpler when she followed her own rules.

But there'd been that moment in his arms, watching him bring her to orgasm....

Simpler was not always better.

"You said that."

"I always mixed up the two. Men and alcohol. There was no way to separate them in my mind. They were two wagons that were hitched together and I couldn't fall off of one without falling off the other."

He nodded. "I can see that."

"Then you come along and you're...all my triggers wrapped up in one gorgeous smile. And I—" Jo swallowed, wishing this were easier. But it wasn't. It wouldn't ever be. "I wasn't strong enough to say no to you. Not the first time."

Phillip spun to face her fully. She could see him trying to understand, trying to make the connection. "You think that sleeping with me will lead to drinking?"

She nodded. "Don't get me wrong. The sex—you were amazing. I'd...I'd forgotten how good it could be. How much I liked it."

"That's a relief." He grinned, but instead of his normal, confident grin, this one seemed a little more unsure. "I thought I'd done something you didn't like."

"Yeah, no—*amazing.*" She shuddered at the memory of his teeth moving against her skin. "But in my mind, I'd fallen off one wagon. I can't afford to fall off the other. What if I lose control? Because then I'll lose everything I've worked for. *Everything.*"

"I understand. Weirdly enough."

She looked at him in surprise. "You do?"

"Look, my six days isn't much on your decade, but... this is *so* much harder than I thought."

She knew that feeling—that the mountain was insurmountable and failure was guaranteed. "*This*," she said, unable to keep the grin off her face, "is the part where I say 'one day at a time.'"

"I don't have to sing 'Kumbaya,' do I?"

She laughed. "God, no."

He came to her then, his arms slipping around her waist. She hugged him back. She couldn't fight this attraction. "Stay with me, Jo. Wake up with me."

"For how long? Sun's getting better. He won't need me much longer."

Phillip stroked his thumb over her cheek. "For as long as you want. Betty loves it here. And I have other horses, if you're worried about missing a job."

A job? No, she wasn't worried about that. She set her own schedule and that schedule could be rearranged. But would she still *get* jobs, if word got around? "I don't want people to know about this. About us. No tweeting or press releases or pictures."

His eyebrows shot up. She kept going before she lost her nerve. "I am a professional. I can't have this compromise my reputation as a trainer."

He nodded. "This has nothing to do with Sun. You've done an amazing job with him. This is between us and us alone."

She swallowed. "What about your club appearances?"

"That's why I hired Fred. He'll be with me any time I have to leave the farm." He stroked the edge of his thumb over her cheek.

They were standing on the edge again, but it felt less like falling off a cliff and more like…falling in love. Which was ridiculous. She'd never been in love. She had no plans to start now. "I thought you weren't seducing me."

He brushed his lips across her forehead. "You can stay in the guest room tonight if you want."

She gave him a look then pulled away from him so she could get her thoughts in order. "I can't put myself at risk for you. If you want to be with me, you have to stay sober." She cupped his face in her hands. "I *cannot* kiss you and taste whiskey. I just can't. It's a deal breaker."

His eyes searched hers. Gone was the haunted, raw pain she'd seen a few days ago. His eyes were clear and bright and filled with a different kind of need. "I'm *done* drinking, Jo."

He kissed her then, rough and gentle at the same time.

She'd already fallen off the man wagon. But that didn't have to mean she'd fall right back into drinking. As long as she kept a hard line between her time with Phillip and alcohol—and they kept a hard wall between what happened in the paddock and what happened in the bedroom—she could indulge in some great safe sex and enjoy herself without repercussions.

She hoped.

Thunder cracked around them. Sun whinnied, but he didn't freak out. "Come up to the house," Phillip murmured as his teeth scraped over the skin where her neck and shoulder joined. "Wake up with me."

Her remaining resolve crumbled. How could she say no to that?

She couldn't.

So she didn't.

Fourteen

The next three weeks were something far outside of Jo's experience. Suddenly, she was living with Phillip Beaumont. She'd never lived with anyone besides her parents and a few unfortunate college roommates.

But this? Waking up with Phillip's arms wrapped around her waist? Making sweet love in the morning, then having breakfast together? Spending the day working with Sun—sometimes with Phillip, sometimes without—then heading back up to the house after the hired help had gone home for the night to have dinner with him? Falling into bed with him at night where he was both rough and gentle in the best possible ways?

It was easy. What's more, it was good. Well, of course the sex was good. But her time with Phillip went well beyond that. Yes, they had sex at least once a day—usually twice. But she got up the next morning, kissed Phillip, and did what she always did—worked with Sun.

After a week, he would come to her to be haltered. After

two, he consented to be tied to the fence so she could brush him. He really was golden, a shimmering color that she'd never seen on a horse before.

She even had Richard walk by a few times while Jo led the horse around the paddock. Sun wasn't happy, but he also wasn't insane with fear.

A new sense of calm filled her. After ten damned long years, she'd managed to unhook the men wagon from the drinking wagon. The realization that she could enjoy Phillip and still be the same woman was—well, it was freeing.

Phillip left the farm after a week and a half. His sober coach showed up at the farm the afternoon Phillip was to leave. Jo stayed with Sun, but she knew that Phillip, Fred and Ortiz were discussing ways they would keep Phillip in control. No drinking, no hook-ups—Phillip had promised—and no blackouts. That was the plan.

Phillip would text her at regular intervals. She could also follow along at home via Twitter, where he'd be posting to his account.

Jo stayed in her trailer, Betty bedded down next to her as she toggled between texts and Twitter, where Phillip shared his Instagram photos. "Can't believe how stupid some people are drunk," he texted her with a photo of a public sex act between two women and one guy.

She smiled at her phone. "Doing okay?"

"Miss you & Betty," was the response. "Home soon."

Later that night, her phone buzzed her out of a dream. It was a photo of Fred in one of two double beds in a hotel room. "Not alone tonight," the text read. "Just me & Fred. He's no Betty, but he'll do. J Miss you."

"Miss you too." She was shocked by how much.

Phillip was back in the paddock by four Sunday afternoon. He'd made it through three events in two days without a drop of liquor. They'd been doing really well about not displaying their affection in front of the hired help, but she didn't stop him when he kissed her for what felt like a good five minutes. When the kiss broke, they realized Sun was watching them.

"Later," she'd giggled. Actually giggled.

"You can bet on it."

"Later" couldn't come fast enough but finally they made it to the bedroom without even eating dinner. After amazing sex where Phillip held her down and left bite marks on her breasts, he said, "I did it," as he lay in her arms, both of them panting and satisfied.

She knew he wasn't talking about the two orgasms that had her body humming. "You did. I knew you could."

He propped himself up on his elbows to look down at her. "You did?"

"No one's past saving."

He lowered himself down onto her. "Who knew being saved could be so good?"

She didn't get a chance to reply.

Phillip was home for another week before he had to go again. This time, he headed to a music festival where Beaumont Brewery had sponsored a party tent. Jo was nervous for him—this wasn't a few hours at a party, but a solid weekend of temptation. But he had Fred and he knew he could do it. So she sent him off with a kiss and the reminder, "Don't forget." She wanted to say more. But she didn't.

"I won't," he promised her. And she believed him.

That Saturday, she had to fight the temptation to check her phone constantly. She'd made it a policy not to check her phone while she was in the paddock with Sun—the horse was smart enough to know when her focus was elsewhere. Distractions were how trainers got hurt. So she left her phone in the trailer. That way, it wouldn't tempt her.

She checked her messages at lunch. Only one text that

read, "Gonna be a long day. Wish I was home with you," that he'd sent at ten that morning. Nothing since.

She swallowed, feeling a kind of anxiety she hadn't felt in a long time—a futility that she couldn't change things so why bother? That'd been the way she used to think when she'd wake up and be confronted with what she'd done. Changing seemed so hard, so impossible—why even try?

Expecting Phillip to change, just like that?

No, wait. No need to jump to conclusions. Phillip had just realized that she'd be working in the paddock all day, that was all. And he was busy doing...party things.

She sent a text—"I know you can do this, babe." Then, she sent another—"Don't forget."

Don't forget me, she wanted to add, but didn't. Instead, she took a quick photo of Sun and sent it.

She didn't get a reply.

What could she do? Nothing. It was not as if she could go to him. He was in Texas. This was up to him. She couldn't make the choice for him, any more than her parents could have kept her from driving to that convenience store.

So she pushed her worry from her mind. She wanted to try and saddle Sun and that required her full attention. But the work didn't stop her from praying that Phillip remembered. Or, at the very least, that Fred forcibly reminded Phillip what was on the line.

Because what was on the line was the farm. The horses. This was about Sun and the Appaloosas and all the Percherons—Beaumont Farms. Not her. What she needed to remember was that she was here for the reference, the paycheck—the prestige of having saved a horse no one else could.

She had to keep up the wall between what happened in the paddock and the bedroom.

But he'd promised her. And she so desperately wanted him to keep that promise.

She didn't get Sun saddled. The horse must have picked up on her nerves because he refused to stand still long enough for her to brush him. She did get him back into his stall. She left Betty in the stall next to him—hopefully that would help him mellow out more.

Then, dread building in her stomach, she went to her trailer and got her phone. No new text messages.

She sat there, her fingers on the buttons. She shouldn't be afraid to look, right? He had Fred. He had a clear head. He wouldn't forget. He wouldn't forget *her*. She was making a mountain out of a molehill. He was working, no doubt. She needed to get a grip.

Fortified by these completely logical thoughts, she toggled over to Twitter—and her stomach immediately fell in. Oh, *no*. He'd posted pictures almost every half hour of him with famous people she recognized and a lot of people she didn't. A lot of women.

The women were concerning—but not nearly as worrisome as the look in Phillip's eyes. As she scrolled through the feed, his eyes got blearier. Each smile stayed the same—infectious and fun-loving—but his eyes? They were flatter and flatter.

What had he done?

Then she saw it. The bottle of Beaumont Beer in his hand, almost hidden behind the waist of a curvaceous redhead. Open.

The next photo, the bottle was less hidden. She needed to stop scrolling, but she couldn't help herself. How far had he fallen? How much had he forgotten?

Everything. The women in the pictures got more outrageous, more hands-on. The beer got more obvious. And the look in Phillip's eyes? He wouldn't remember any of this.

And she knew that she'd never forget it.

Each picture after that was worse until she got to the photos he'd posted about an hour ago. She knew the guys in the photo were some famous band, but she didn't know which one. All she knew was that they were surrounding Phillip on stage and they were toasting with their beer bottles. Phillip toasted with them.

After that, she shut her phone off and sat there, staring at the dinette tabletop. This *feeling* of hopelessness, helplessness—this was exactly why she'd held herself back. She'd always told herself it was to keep people safe, like Tony, the guy who'd died in a car next to her. She couldn't get involved with people because it would end badly for them. And there was no question that this would end badly for Phillip.

But he'd made his choice. He could drink away his pain.

She couldn't. That hard wall she'd demanded between men and alcohol—between Phillip and whiskey—she had to cling to that wall.

She never should have slept with him. Cared about him. Fallen for him.

Because now she was going to hurt. And just like the pain she'd had to feel when she'd been coming out of surgeries and physical therapy, she'd have to feel all of this.

She didn't want to. God, she didn't want to hurt, to know she'd broken her own rules and now she was going to pay the price for it.

Her mind spun, trying to find something that would allow her to sidestep around the heartache. Okay, Phillip had fallen off the wagon. Everyone did, right? Obviously, there'd been a problem with the sober coach because he hadn't been in any of the pictures. Fred had screwed up. They'd fire Fred, wherever he was, and hire another sober coach. Someone who wouldn't bail on Phillip in high-pressure situations. This could be fixed. This could be...

Against her will, she picked up her phone. A new picture popped up. Phillip, with his arms around two women who could have been the same two he'd brought to the ranch a month ago. He had a bottle in each hand. His lips were pressed against the cheek of one of the women.

No, it couldn't be fixed. She was making excuses for him and she knew it. They'd had a deal. She couldn't be with him if he wasn't sober. She couldn't kiss him and taste whiskey.

Whatever Fred did or did not do, it still came down to Phillip. It was his call. He'd gone to this event just like she'd driven herself to that gas station all those years ago. He'd been faced with a beer tent, just like she'd stood in front of the walls of cans.

She'd walked away from beer. She'd stayed on the wagon.

He hadn't.

Phillip was an alcoholic. And he was, at this very moment, drunk and probably getting drunker. She'd told him she couldn't be the reason he chose to stay sober. She'd meant it every single time she'd said it.

It shouldn't have hurt so much. But it did. God, it did.

She couldn't save Phillip if he didn't want her to. And to stay around him when he had whiskey on his breath.... He'd tempt her.

Could she really stop kissing him? Could she really stop loving him?

She couldn't. It was all or nothing with her. Always had been. And once she tasted that whiskey...

She rubbed at the skin on the back of her neck. The deal was broken. In so many ways.

What did that leave her with? Besides a broken heart?

It was time to go. She'd done her job. Sun could be haltered, moved and brushed without causing harm to himself or anyone else. The horse, at least, was on the road to recovery.

She *had* to leave before Phillip took her down with him.

She'd left jobs before. Leaving shouldn't be the hard part. Except…she'd started to think of the Beaumont Farms as home. Betty loved it here. Betty and Sun were friends.

She just…she needed another job. Something new to focus on. Something to remind her who she was and what she wanted. She was a horse trainer. One of the best. She didn't need friends or…love.

It just caused pain and since she was an alcoholic, she couldn't ever take anything to numb it. The high wasn't worth it. It wasn't worth *this*.

The only thing she had was her work and her rules. Rules she wouldn't bend, much less break, ever again.

She opened her laptop and blindly scrolled through emails about damaged horses, only to find herself typing a message to her parents. "*Coming home*," she wrote. "*I didn't forget*."

It was only then that she realized she was crying.

Fifteen

Everything moved, including Phillip's stomach. *Urgh.*

Jo. He needed Jo. Jo would make this better.

He was moving. Why was he moving? He tried to open his eyes, but it didn't work, so he patted around with his hands.

God, his head. Why did it hurt so badly? Combined with the moving...his stomach was going to make him pay.

He hit something cool and round and long. A bottle. Why was there a bottle next to him on the seat?

Everything shifted to the right and the bottle rolled away. It made the dull clanking noise of glass bouncing off glass. The noise did horrible things to his head.

But he managed to get his eyes open. He was in his limo. He thought. Except...there were bottles everywhere. His fingers closed around something soft and lacy. He held up a scrap of fabric and stared at it for a minute before he realized that it was a pair of red panties. Not the kind Jo wore.

Oh, *shit*. He dropped them as if they were poison and stared around the limo. There were beer bottles all over the place and a few other scraps of clothing. And a woman's shoe. And some questionable stains. God, the *smell*. What had happened?

Oh, no. *No*.

He needed fresh air right now. He fumbled for the knobs on the door. His window went down, which let in way too much light. What time was it?

When was it?

He didn't know. He didn't know where he was or where Jo was and he didn't know what he'd done. But the limo—the limo was full of answers. The wrong ones.

That realization made him want to throw up.

He reached for his phone, but it wasn't there. He tried the knobs again and this time, the divider between the front and the back of the limo slid down.

"Mr. Beaumont? Is everything all right?"

"Uh…" He tried to think, but damn his head. "Ortiz?"

"Yes, Mr. Beaumont?"

"Where are we?"

"We'll be at the farm in ten minutes, Mr. Beaumont."

The farm. Jo. He needed her. Oh, God, she was going to be so mad. "What…time is it?"

"Four. In the afternoon," Ortiz helpfully added.

"Sunday?"

"Sunday."

That meant he hadn't missed that day. Just…Phillip rubbed his head, which did not help. Did he remember Saturday?

"What happened to Fred?"

"He was arrested."

That sounded bad. "Why?"

"He punched Pitbull—you know, the rapper?" Ortiz waited for some sign of recognition, but Phillip had nothing. Ortiz sighed. "There was a fight and Fred got arrested."

"I don't…" *I don't remember.* But that was probably obvious at this point. "Is he still in jail?"

Ortiz shook his head, which somehow made Phillip dizzy. "Your brother Mr. Matthew Beaumont bailed him out."

"Oh." That wasn't his fault, was it? If Fred got arrested and left him all alone, that wasn't his doing, right? He needed to send a message to Jo. He needed to tell her he hadn't done it on purpose. Any of it. It'd just been…it'd been a mistake. Everyone made them. He patted his pocket for his phone, but it still wasn't there. "Where's my phone?"

"It got…flushed. At least, that's what you told me." Ortiz looked at him in the rearview mirror.

"Oh. Right. I remember," he lied. Bad. Very bad.

He really was going to be sick.

Just then, they drove through the massive gates at the edge of Beaumont Farms. His heart tried to feel light—he loved coming back to this place—but there was no lightness in his soul.

He'd messed up. The blackout wasn't worth it.

But it wasn't his fault! Fred was supposed to be his sober coach and he'd gotten in a fight with a rapper and gotten hauled off to jail.

He just had to explain it to Jo, that was all. This was an accident.

He hadn't meant to drink. Bits and pieces filtered back into his consciousness. Fred had disappeared. Phillip had been onstage. Someone had put a beer in his hand. But he wasn't going to drink it. He remembered that clearly now. He wasn't going to drink that beer. He'd promised. He'd hold it, because that was his job. He wanted everyone else to drink Beaumont Beer and have fun. He did a good job. He always did.

But the beer…it'd smelled good. And some woman had kissed him, rubbing her body against his. Because he was Phillip Beaumont and that's what women did. And he *knew* that the picture would wind up online. And that Jo would see it. She'd see this strange woman who meant nothing to him kissing him and the beer bottle in his hand and Jo would think he'd failed her. She'd leave him.

Suddenly, he'd felt the same way he'd felt when Chadwick had said he was selling the farm and the horses—hopeless. He'd been good for three weeks, with Jo, but the moment things went wrong, he wound up with a beer in his hand and woman in his arms. Because it would never change. He would never change.

And the woman tasted like beer and he'd liked it. *Needed* it. Needed not to think about how Jo would look at him, the disappointment all over her.

There'd been a bottle in his hand….

And he'd stopped thinking. Stopped feeling.

"Mr. Beaumont, you want to go to the house?"

What had he done? He *needed* Jo. He needed that silly little donkey. He needed someone to tell him that it would be okay, that he could sleep it off and tomorrow they'd go back to normal. The farm. The horses. Sun. Tomorrow, this would all be a bad dream.

He needed to see her and know that she forgave him. That he hadn't disappointed her. That he hadn't forgotten her, not really.

"The white barn." Yeah, he probably looked like hell and smelled worse, but he had to talk to Jo *now*.

They drove through the perfect pastures. His horses trotted in the fields. It was perfect.

Except for the big trailer hitched to a truck out front. No, no, *no*. He'd gotten here just in time. She couldn't leave. She couldn't leave *him*.

Ortiz pulled off a few feet opposite the trailer. Phillip

tried to open the door but he missed the handle the first time. Then the door swung open and Ortiz was hauling him out. "You sure you want to do this, boss?"

Phillip winced at the sound. "Gotta talk to her." He tried to pull free, but the world started rolling, so he let Ortiz hold him up.

They awkwardly started toward her trailer. He didn't need Ortiz. He could walk. He stopped and straightened up, but his feet wouldn't cooperate. He stumbled and went down to one knee.

"Mr. Beaumont," Ortiz said. "Please."

Phillip heard noises but he couldn't make out what they were. Then he was on his feet again. His head rolled to one side and he saw that Richard was under his left side. "Dick?"

"Don't know if you realize this, sir, but you only call me Dick when you're drunk."

"Wasn't my fault," Phillip tried.

"Sure it wasn't. Let's get you to the house."

"No—need Jo. Betty?"

"*Sir*," Richard said in a voice that was too loud for everything. Then they started moving. Away from the barn. Away from the trailer.

"Wait," came a different voice. A female voice.

Jo.

Somehow, Phillip got himself turned around and found himself facing Jo. This turned out not to be a good thing.

The woman he'd spent weeks chasing? Gone. The chase was over. He could see it in her eyes—hard and cold.

Next to her stood Betty, her small body wrapped up in something that had to be a harness.

"No." It came out shaky. Weak. He tried to clear his throat and start again. "Don't go. I'm sorry."

"Sun," Jo said, "is manageable. He can be haltered and

walked from the stall to the paddock. He can be brushed. He's doing much better."

That statement hung in the air. Phillip was pretty sure he heard someone else whisper "unlike you" but every time he tried to move his head, he had to fight off nausea.

"I didn't—Fred—*Jo*," he begged. Why weren't the words there? Why couldn't he say the right things to make her stay? "Don't go. I'm sorry. I'll do better. I'll *be* better. For you."

Jo looked at the men on either side of Phillip. Both of them stepped back and, miracle of miracles, Phillip's legs held. He stood before her. It was all he could do.

"No. Not *for* me." She took a step toward him. "We had a deal, you and I." This time, her voice was softer. Sadder.

"It won't happen again. Don't leave me. I can't do this without you."

She reached up, her palm warm and soft against his cheek. He leaned into her touch so much he almost lost his balance.

"I can't kiss you and taste whiskey. I can't be the reason you drink or don't drink. I never could. I can't..." She swallowed then, closing her eyes as if she was digging deep for something. "I can't love you more than you love the bottle. So I won't."

Love. That was a good word. The best one he had. "I love you, Jo. Don't go."

Her smile wasn't one, not really. Not when tears spilled down her cheeks. "I won't forget our time together, Phillip." She leaned in close, her breath warming his cheek. "I won't forget you. I just wish...I wish you could say the same."

He tried to put his arms around her and hold onto her until she stopped saying she was leaving, but she was gone—away from him, picking up Betty off the ground and cradling her in her arms.

"No," he tried, but his voice didn't seem to be working so well. "Don't." He tried to chase after her, but he tripped and went down to his knees again. *"Don't."*

Then people were holding him back—or up, or both— he didn't know. All he knew was that she walked away from him.

She carried Betty to her truck. She got in. The door shut. She drove away.

After that, he didn't remember anything else.

He didn't want to.

Sixteen

Jo dusted off her chaps as she climbed back to her feet. Precious was not in the mood to run barrels right now. Jo sighed. If a horse could be passive aggressive, Precious was. She'd let Jo saddle her and mount up as if they were old friends and then *boom*. Jo was on the ground and Precious was on the other side of the paddock, munching grass.

Jo glared as she walked over to the horse. "Here's the bad news," she said as she grabbed the reins and wiped the sweat from her eyes. Late summer sun beat down on her head. Not for the first time, she missed the cool greenness of Beaumont Farms, even as she tried to tell herself that it was summer there, too. "That worked for about twelve seconds. Now we're going to do it again and again until you get tired of it."

Precious shook her head and tried to back up.

Oh, no—Jo wasn't having any of that. She swung into the saddle before the horse could get very far. This time, Jo

was ready for her and managed to stay in the saddle when
Precious went sideways. "Ha!" she said as she guided the
horse around the makeshift barrel run she'd set up in her
parents' paddock. "Again."

They ran the barrels several more times, Precious trying to buck her off at the same spot each time. Jo held on.
The less fun the horse could have bucking her off, the more
likely she'd stop doing it.

In the two months since she'd come home, Jo had continued to train horses. She'd given up the road—for the
time being, at least. She was back in her room and her mom
was back to grumbling about a donkey sliding around on
the hallway rugs.

It'd taken a few days, but Jo had finally told her granny
what had happened as they'd rocked on the porch swing.

"Be thankful for the rain," Lina had said after Jo had
cried on her shoulder. Which was a very Lina thing to say.
"Nothing grows, nothing moves forward without a little
rain now and then."

Which was all well and good, except Jo didn't feel as if
she'd grown much at all. She was still living with her parents, though that was her choice. She'd billed Beaumont
Farms for the time she'd spent with Sun and received a
check signed by Matthew Beaumont.

The check alone was enough for a down payment on a
piece of land. She could have her pick of properties any-
where she wanted to stake her claim.

But she hadn't pulled the trigger on anything yet. It'd
been a relief to come home, to be surrounded by people
who loved her no matter what. People who didn't think
she'd done the stupid thing by walking away from Phillip
Beaumont, but the smart thing.

Plus, after a few months at Beaumont Farms, nothing
seemed quite good enough.

She told herself that she was just taking some time off,

but that wasn't true, either. She'd had five horses delivered to her on the ranch, including Precious.

At least she was still getting jobs. Because Phillip had so spectacularly come apart, her leaving the job as she did—crying—had not come back to bite her on the butt. She didn't know what people might be saying about her and Phillip, but it hadn't impacted her work. She was still, first and foremost, a horse trainer who used "nontraditional" methods. Desperate horse owners still wanted her to save their horses. That was a good thing. It paid the bills.

She could be back on the road anytime she wanted to go. And now, she knew she would not have moments of weakness, moments of need. The walls she'd built up—for her own good—would stay up. No more Phillip. No more men. She'd gotten used to it once. She'd get used to it again.

She needed to get used to waking up alone, to going to sleep the same way. To frustrated sexual desire that she was having trouble burying like she used to.

She'd made it years without a man. It'd just take a little while to work Phillip out of her system, that was all. Once she was sure she could do fine on her own again, she'd load up her trailer and hit the road. She'd start looking for a place then.

She spent another hour with Precious, managing to stay in the saddle the whole time. Jo was about to call it a day when she saw a plume of dust kicking up down the road.

She looked back at the house. No one had mentioned they were expecting company today and Precious's owner wasn't due back until this weekend. Who would be driving this far out to the middle of nowhere?

As the car got closer, she saw it was an extended-cab, dual-wheeled truck—a lot like the one she used to haul her trailer. Must be a fellow rancher coming to talk to Dad, she reasoned as she pulled the saddle off Precious and began rubbing the horse down.

She heard the truck stop behind her, heard boots on gravel. "Dad's in the house," she called over her shoulder.

Then she heard Betty braying in the way she did when she was excited about something.

"Hey, Betty—you remember me? That's a good girl."

Jo froze, brush hovering over Precious's back. She knew that voice.

Phillip.

She turned slowly. Phillip Beaumont stood halfway between the truck and the paddock. He was wearing broken-in jeans and a button up shirt that walked the fine line between cowboy and hipster. The tips of brown boots were barely visible in the dirt.

He was rubbing Betty's ears. The donkey leaned into his legs as if the two of them had never been apart.

Something in Jo's chest clenched. He was here. It'd been almost two months, but he was here *now.*

Then he looked up at her. His eyes were brighter, the green in them greener. He looked good. Better than good. He looked right, like the true version of himself.

She was *so* glad to see him. She didn't want to be— she was getting him out of her system—but she was. God, she was.

Behind him, a small man wearing wire-rim glasses stepped out from the other side of the truck.

Phillip nodded his head to the man. "This is Dale," he said with no other introduction. "He's been my sober companion since I got out of rehab."

She should not be this glad to see him. It didn't matter to her one way or the other what he did or why he did it. But still… "You were in rehab?"

"Twenty-eight days in Malibu. I've been sober for fifty-three days now." He gave her a crooked grin, as if this statistic was something that he was both proud of and embarrassed by.

"You have?" She stared at him—and got hip-checked by Precious. She stumbled forward and turned to glare at the horse. "One second," she told Phillip and Dale.

She untied Precious's lead from the fence and opened the paddock gate. It didn't take longer than a minute or two to lead the horse to a pasture, but it felt as if it took a week. She felt Phillip's eyes on her the entire time and, just as it had that first time, it made her want to flutter.

She wanted to throw herself in his arms and tell him how damn much she'd missed him—missed working horses with him, missed waking up with him.

Things she couldn't miss. Things she *wouldn't* miss.

He was just a temptation, that was all. And she'd gotten very good at resisting temptations. Was this any different than standing in front of the beer coolers in a convenience store?

No. She was strong enough to resist.

Once the horse was turned loose, she faced Phillip again. "You finished rehab and have been sober for almost two months?"

"I knew you might not believe me." But instead of being put out by her doubt, Phillip's eyes focused on hers as if no one else in the world existed. "That's why I brought Dale. He can vouch for me."

She looked at Dale, who nodded. "He's followed his plan perfectly."

"You have a plan?" They'd had a plan before and that hadn't worked out so well. "What happened?"

Phillip took a step toward her. The confident grin was gone and he looked earnest. She wanted to believe him. Oh, how she wanted to believe him.

"I believe the correct phrase is 'hit bottom.' Matthew took me to rehab three days after you left. It wasn't exactly fun, but after my head cleared, I knew I could do it because I'd already done it with you."

Three days was a long time to bounce around at rock bottom. "And after that? Did you lose the farm?"

He took another step toward her. She wanted to reach out and touch him, to know that he was really here and whole and sober.

"The Beaumont Brewery has been sold. The deal closed. I was able to buy the horses with my share of the sale."

"Just the horses? But the farm..." The farm was his home.

For such a short time, the farm had felt like *her* home.

Another step forward. "Chadwick kept it."

"Oh."

Another step closer. He reached out and brushed his thumb over her cheek. "I no longer work for Beaumont Brewery," Phillip said, cupping her cheek in his hand. "After that last festival, well, we mutually agreed to part company. I have a new job."

"Doing what?"

This step brought him close enough that she could wrap her arms around his waist and hold on to him. She almost did, too. But she couldn't. She *wouldn't*.

"I'm the head of Beaumont Farms."

She blinked up at him. "You're *what?*"

"It turns out that the new owners of the Beaumont Brewery have decided that the Percheron draft team is too valuable to the brand to give up. They're leasing the Percherons from the Beaumont family. Chadwick got them to sign a ten-year non-exclusive contract."

"It worked? Going on the morning shows? The Facebook poll?"

He nodded. "It did. Plus, it turns out that Chadwick is keeping the Percheron Drafts craft beer brand for himself—he's going to use the Percherons, too. The Brewery had exclusive use of the Beaumont wagons and harnesses, but I've been working with Chadwick and Matthew on a marketing plan that will make the best use of the horses while differentiating between the companies."

"Wow. But—Percheron Drafts is still a beer company."

"I don't work for Percheron Drafts. I work for Beaumont Farms. Chadwick incorporated the land as a separate entity. Right now, I *choose* not to visit the new brewery. Chadwick and Matthew have been coming out to the farmhouse for our meetings. They're being extremely supportive."

"Even Chadwick?"

His smile—God, that was going to be her undoing. "Even Chadwick. It turns out that we get along a lot better when I'm not drunk and he's not a jerk."

He leaned down closer—too close. She pulled back, away from his sure hands and intent gaze. "That's really good. I'm happy for you. But why are you here?"

The space she'd put between them wasn't enough to stop the corner of his mouth from curving into a smile that wasn't quite predatory but came damned close. "Because I learned the hard way the blackouts weren't worth it. They weren't worth losing the farm and the horses and they most especially weren't worth losing you. I had a good month where you showed me that my life could be what I wanted it to be. I almost threw it all away. The choice was mine and so was the blame."

She shook her head. He was saying all the right things, all the things she needed to hear. But…

"I can't be the reason, Phillip."

For the first time, she saw doubt in his eyes. "I know. But it turns out, I couldn't live with myself for letting you go."

"You couldn't?"

"No." He took a deep breath. "I'm sorry that I broke my promise to you. I know I hurt you."

"You did. And worse, you made me doubt myself." He

nodded. No lame excuses, no blaming others. He took full responsibility. "But," she went on, "you also showed me that I was stronger than I gave myself credit for."

"Got your wagons unhitched now?"

She couldn't help herself. She smiled at him and was rewarded with a smile of his own. It wasn't fair for a man to look that good. It just wasn't. "Yup."

"Let me make it up to you, Jo. I want to make things right between us."

She eyed him. "How?"

There was that grin again—sharp and confident, a man who always got what he wanted. Even if he had to go through rehab to get it.

"As the manager of Beaumont Farms, I'm looking for ways to make Beaumont the premiere name in the horse world. I happen to have a well-trained stallion that's going to command huge stud fees, but I want to branch out."

Was he calling Sun well-trained? Her face grew hot. "Yeah?"

He nodded, warming to his subject. "I decided having a professional on-site trainer, someone who specializes in rehabilitating broken horses, would add a lot of validity to the brand."

Her mouth dropped open in shock. "You decided *that?*"

He cupped her face in his hands. "Come home to the farm, Jo. I want you. I don't want to lose you again. And I don't want to stay sober *because* of you. I want to do it *for* you. To show you that I'm the man who's not perfect, but perfect for you. Because with you, I'm the man I always wanted to be."

"I can't be with you if you drink. I can't kiss you and taste whiskey. Not now, not ever."

He leaned down, his lips brushing over hers. She was powerless to stop him, powerless to do anything but wrap her arms around his waist and pull him in tight.

"I will never drink again, Jo—because more than the horses, more than the land, I can't lose you. You make me chase you. You never pull your punches with me. I'm not a Beaumont when I'm with you. I'm just Phillip."

"You've always been more than a Beaumont to me," she told him. Her voice came out shaky, but she didn't care.

"I don't want to forget you," he whispered. "I *never* want to forget you."

She crushed her lips against his. His teeth scraped over her lip—rough, but gentle. Just the way she wanted it. Just the way she wanted *him*.

He rested his forehead against hers. Her hat fell off, but she didn't care.

"Don't give up on us. I can't fix what I did, but what we have is worth saving. Marry me, Jo. Come home."

Home. With Phillip. A piece of land she could call her own—*their* own. Everything she'd ever wanted.

"I couldn't forget you, either. I tried. I kept telling myself I just had to get you out of my system, but…"

He grinned, satisfied and hungry all at the same time. One of his fingers traced the spot where her neck met her shoulder. Her body ached for his touch, his bite. "Marry me. We'll remember the days—*and* the nights—together."

How could she say no to that?

She couldn't.

So she didn't.

* * * * *

If you loved TEMPTED BY A COWBOY,
Don't miss the rest of
THE BEAUMONT HEIRS *trilogy!*

NOT THE BOSS'S BABY
Available now

A BEAUMONT CHRISTMAS WEDDING
Available November 2014

From Sarah M. Anderson and Harlequin Desire!

COMING NEXT MONTH FROM

Available November 4, 2014

#2335 THE COWBOY'S PRIDE AND JOY
Billionaires and Babies • by Maureen Child
A wealthy rancher who loves his reclusive mountain, Jake never could resist Cassidy. Especially not when she introduces him to his infant son...just as a snowstorm forces them to face everything that's still between them...

#2336 SHELTERED BY THE MILLIONAIRE
Texas Cattleman's Club: After the Storm • by Catherine Mann
An unexpected passion ignites between single mom and conservationist Megan and her adversarial neighbor. But when she learns the real estate magnate threatens what she's trying to protect, she has to decide—trust the facts...or her heart?

#2337 FROM ENEMY'S DAUGHTER TO EXPECTANT BRIDE
The Billionaires of Black Castle • by Olivia Gates
Rafael Salazar is poised to destroy the man who stole his childhood, but his feelings for his enemy's daughter may threaten his plans. When she becomes pregnant, will he have to choose between revenge and love?

#2338 A BEAUMONT CHRISTMAS WEDDING
The Beaumont Heirs • by Sarah M. Anderson
As best man and a PR specialist, Matthew Beaumont needs his brother's Christmas wedding to be perfect. Then former wild child Whitney Maddox becomes a bridesmaid. Will she ruin the wedding? Or will Matthew discover the real woman behind the celebrity facade?

#2339 THE BOSS'S MISTLETOE MANEUVERS
by Linda Thomas-Sundstrom
Chad goes undercover at the agency he bought to oversee a Christmas campaign. But when the star ad exec with a strange aversion to the holiday jeopardizes the project, Chad doesn't know whether to fire her or seduce her!

#2340 HER DESERT KNIGHT
by Jennifer Lewis
The last thing Dani needs after her divorce is an affair with a man from the family that's been feuding with hers for decades. But notorious seducer Quasar may be the only man who can reawaken her body...and her heart.

REQUEST YOUR FREE BOOKS!
2 FREE NOVELS PLUS 2 FREE GIFTS!

H HARLEQUIN® *Desire*

ALWAYS POWERFUL, PASSIONATE AND PROVOCATIVE

YES! Please send me 2 FREE Harlequin Desire® novels and my 2 FREE gifts (gifts are worth about $10). After receiving them, if I don't wish to receive any more books, I can return the shipping statement marked "cancel." If I don't cancel, I will receive 6 brand-new novels every month and be billed just $4.55 per book in the U.S. or $4.99 per book in Canada. That's a savings of at least 13% off the cover price! It's quite a bargain! Shipping and handling is just 50¢ per book in the U.S. and 75¢ per book in Canada.* I understand that accepting the 2 free books and gifts places me under no obligation to buy anything. I can always return a shipment and cancel at any time. Even if I never buy another book, the two free books and gifts are mine to keep forever.

225/326 HDN F4ZC

Name	(PLEASE PRINT)

Address	Apt. #

City	State/Prov.	Zip/Postal Code

Signature (if under 18, a parent or guardian must sign)

Mail to the **Harlequin® Reader Service:**

IN U.S.A.: P.O. Box 1867, Buffalo, NY 14240-1867
IN CANADA: P.O. Box 609, Fort Erie, Ontario L2A 5X3

Want to try two free books from another line?
Call 1-800-873-8635 or visit www.ReaderService.com.

* Terms and prices subject to change without notice. Prices do not include applicable taxes. Sales tax applicable in N.Y. Canadian residents will be charged applicable taxes. Offer not valid in Quebec. This offer is limited to one order per household. Not valid for current subscribers to Harlequin Desire books. All orders subject to credit approval. Credit or debit balances in a customer's account(s) may be offset by any other outstanding balance owed by or to the customer. Please allow 4 to 6 weeks for delivery. Offer available while quantities last.

Your Privacy—The Harlequin® Reader Service is committed to protecting your privacy. Our Privacy Policy is available online at www.ReaderService.com or upon request from the Harlequin Reader Service.

We make a portion of our mailing list available to reputable third parties that offer products we believe may interest you. If you prefer that we not exchange your name with third parties, or if you wish to clarify or modify your communication preferences, please visit us at www.ReaderService.com/consumerschoice or write to us at Harlequin Reader Service Preference Service, P.O. Box 9062, Buffalo, NY 14269. Include your complete name and address.

HD13R

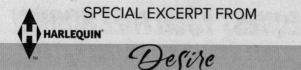
Here's a sneak peek at the next scandalous Beaumont
Heirs book,

A BEAUMONT CHRISTMAS WEDDING
By Sarah M. Anderson

Available November 2014 from Harlequin® Desire.

What if Matthew Beaumont could look at her without
caring about who she'd been in the past?

What if—what if he wasn't involved with anyone?

Whitney didn't hook up. That part of her life was dead
and buried. But…a little Christmas romance between the
maid of honor and the best man wouldn't be such a bad
thing, would it? It could be fun.

She hurried to the bathroom, daring to hope that
Matthew was single. He was coming to dinner tonight
and it sounded as if he would be involved with a lot of the
wedding activities.

Although…it had been a long time since she'd attempted
anything involving the opposite sex. Making a pass at the
best man might not be the smartest thing she could do.

Even so, Whitney went with the red cashmere sweater—
the kind a single, handsome man might accidentally brush
with his fingers—and headed out. The house had hallways
in all directions, and she was relieved when she heard
voices—Jo's and Phillip's and another voice, deep and
strong. Matthew.

She hurried down the steps, then remembered she was trying to make a good impression. She slowed too quickly and stumbled. Hard. She braced for the impact.

It didn't come. Instead of hitting the floor, she fell into a pair of strong arms and against a firm, warm chest.

Whitney looked up into a pair of eyes that were deep blue. He smiled down at her and she didn't feel as if she was going to forget her own name. She felt as if she'd never forget this moment.

"I've got you."

He did have her. His arms were around her waist and he was lifting her up. She felt secure.

The feeling was *wonderful*.

Then, without warning, everything changed. His warm smile froze as his eyes went hard. The strong arms became iron bars around her and the next thing she knew, she was being pushed not up, but away.

Matthew Beaumont set her back on her feet and stepped clear of her. With a glare that could only be described as ferocious, he turned to Phillip and Jo.

"What," he said, "is Whitney Wildz doing here?"

Don't miss
A BEAUMONT CHRISTMAS WEDDING
By Sarah M. Anderson

Available November 2014 from Harlequin® Desire.

HARLEQUIN®

Desire

POWERFUL HEROES... SCANDALOUS SECRETS... BURNING DESIRES!

**Explore the new tantalizing story from
the *Texas Cattleman's Club: After the Storm* series**

SHELTERED BY THE MILLIONAIRE

by *USA TODAY* bestselling author
Catherine Mann

As a Texas town rebuilds, love heals all wounds....

Texas tycoon Drew Farrell has always been a thorn in
Beth Andrews's side, especially when he puts the kibosh
on her animal shelter. But when he saves her daughter
during the worst tornado in recent memory, Beth sees
beneath his prickly exterior to the hero underneath.
Soon, the storm's recovery makes bedfellows of these
opposites. Until Beth's old reflexes kick in—should she
brace for betrayal or say yes to Drew once and for all?

Available **NOVEMBER 2014**
wherever books and ebooks are sold.

Talk to us online!
www.Facebook.com/HarlequinBooks
www.Pinterest.com/HarlequinBooks
www.Twitter.com/HarlequinBooks